TED RUSHGROVE

DOC DRYDEN, GUNSLINGER

Complete and Unabridged

LINFORD
Leicester

First published in Great Britain in 2010 by
Robert Hale Limited, London

First Linford Edition
published 2011
by arrangement with
Robert Hale Limited, London

The moral right of the author has been asserted

British Library CIP Data

Rushgrove, Ted.
  Doc Dryden, gunslinger. – –
(Linford western library)
1. Physicians- -Fiction
2. Brothers- -Death- -Fiction.
3. Western stories.
4. Large type books.
I. Title II. Series
823.9′2–dc22

ISBN 978–1–4448–0763–9

Published by
F. A. Thorpe (Publishing)
Anstey, Leicestershire

Set by Words & Graphics Ltd.
Anstey, Leicestershire
Printed and bound in Great Britain by
T. J. International Ltd., Padstow, Cornwall

This book is printed on acid-free paper

DOC DRYDEN, GUNSLINGER

Clay Dryden, one of the band of outlaws known as the Sankey gang, is challenged to a gunfight by the brother of the gang leader and kills him. Finding that there were no bullets in his brother's revolver, Sankey vows to avenge his death. Then, in the town of Crossville, Sankey finds the former outlaw has set up a medical practice. Will Dryden be spared? It seems that Clay's future as the town's doctor hangs in the balance . . .

Books by Ted Rushgrove
in the Linford Western Library:

WAGONS ROLL

1

A tall stranger walked into the bar of the Three Horseshoes saloon. His weather-beaten face was unremarkable, being neither particularly handsome nor ugly. His fair hair was combed back from his wide forehead. His best features were his eyes which were a rather unusual pale blue. The bartender, whose name was Sam, guessed the stranger's age at around thirty. Sam always prided himself on being able to guess people's ages, and being accurate most of the time.

The bar was fairly empty at that time of the day. Just the usual card school, another small band of cowboys playing quoits, and a couple of regulars who were propping up the bar. Later, when the Irish navvies who were building the railway came in, things would change. Instead of being a comparatively quiet

1

retreat, the bar would become a noisier place.

'What can I get for you?' Sam asked the question which he had asked hundreds of times in the past.

'I'll have a beer.' As Sam pulled the beer, the stranger added: 'Will you have one yourself?'

'Thanks.' Sam hadn't had a drink for a couple of hours. He usually paced himself so that he had half a dozen drinks in the evening.

The stranger leaned on the bar and sipped his beer. 'It's quiet here,' he observed.

'It won't be when the Irishmen arrive,' Sam replied.

'Ah, they're building the railway, I assume,' said the stranger.

'That's right. The railway is coming to Crossville at last. They've been talking about it for years. But as you can see if you rode in from Fort Munro it's definitely on its way at last.'

'I came in the other way. From Bircher,' supplied the stranger, taking another pull on his beer.

'They say everything will change in the town once the railway arrives,' said Sam. 'It made a big difference to Fort Munro. They've even got an opera house.'

'You'll probably get more customers at this time of the day,' suggested the stranger.

One of the card-players came up to the bar to replenish his glass. He overheard the remark. 'An opera house is the last thing we need in Crossville,' he stated. 'We've got a brothel already. We'll stick to that.' The other card-players laughed appreciatively.

'You don't let out rooms, do you?' enquired the stranger.

'No,' replied Sam. 'But if you're looking for rooms I can recommend Mrs Neal. She's a widow who lives in the street behind the livery stable.'

'Thanks. I'll give her a call,' came the reply.

At that moment a pretty brunette entered the bar. She nodded to Sam, gave the stranger a smile and went up to the piano which stood in the corner on a rostrum.

She rummaged through some music scores which were on top of the piano. She found what she wanted and began to play.

She hummed the tune as she played. When she had finished she turned round. 'Does anybody know this song?' she demanded.

Her question was met with silence from the card-players.

'Do you know it?' she addressed the remark to the stranger.

'It's the *Londonderry Air*. Its popular name is *Danny Boy*.'

'That's right. It's an Irish song. It should please the Irishmen when they come in later in the week.'

The singer carried on thumbing through some songs while the stranger asked Sam to pour out another couple of drinks.

'I'll give this round a miss, thanks,' replied Sam. 'Are you a musician?' he demanded. 'You knew the tune that Milly was playing.'

'I used to play a trumpet,' replied the stranger. 'I must have heard the song somewhere along the way.'

Shortly afterwards he finished his drink. 'I'll call in to see Mrs Neal,' he informed Sam.

'As far as I know she's still got an empty room to let. By the way, if you come in here again, what do I call you?'

The stranger hesitated for a second. Then he gave his name. 'Clay Dryden.'

Sam waited until he had gone out through the swing door. Then he turned to Milly who had come up to the bar.

'Did you see that?'

'What?' she replied, innocently.

'The guy didn't give me his name straight away.'

'Maybe he had some reason for keeping it to himself.'

'Or maybe it isn't his real name,' said Sam, suggestively.

2

Mrs Neal looked Clay up and down before inviting him inside her cottage.

'You can't be too careful who you let into your house these days,' she informed him as she ushered him into a small parlour.

Clay had already explained that the bartender of the Three Horseshoes saloon had advised him to call since she might have lodgings available.

'We get a lot of undesirables around here these days,' she said, warming to her original theme. 'They say they're coming into town because it's going to become a boom town once the railway arrives. You're nothing to do with the railway, are you?' she concluded.

Clay smiled. 'No, I've got nothing to do with the railway. Except that I travel on it now and then.'

'You do a lot of travelling, Mr . . . ?'

'The name's Clay Dryden. I'm generally known as Clay. Yes, I've travelled quite a bit.'

'So how long will you want the room for?'

'To start with a month. But if things work out I'll be staying longer.'

'A month to start will be all right. I charge seven dollars a week. You'll get one hot meal in the evening at seven o'clock. I hope you don't drink too much.'

'A pint or two is my usual limit.'

'I'm glad to hear it. They say drunkenness will increase when the Irishmen come into town.'

'I expect working on the railway is thirsty work,' stated Clay.

'Well, anyway it will be nice when it's all completed and they've moved on. Now, I'll show you up to your room.'

She led the way up a narrow staircase to the back bedroom. It was a neat room with a wool rug, a double bed, a dressing-table and a wardrobe.

'I hope you'll be comfortable here,' she fussed.

'It looks perfect,' said Clay, taking out his wallet. 'If I pay you a week in advance, will that be all right?'

'Yes, that will be fine, Mr Dryden.'

'Call me Clay,' came the reply.

'If you don't mind I'll call you by your surname. It's a practice I've always adopted with my lodgers.'

Although Mrs Neal didn't want to get too familiar with her lodgers by calling them by their first name, it didn't mean any lack of interest on her part in their activities.

It was obvious from the way that Dryden had opened his wallet that he wasn't short of money. The wallet had been full of five-dollar bills. Dryden had paid her with one and added two silver dollars.

Although he was weather-beaten he didn't appear to be someone who worked on a ranch. She had especially noticed his hands when he had taken the money from his wallet. They were not the gnarled hands of a manual worker. In fact they were the hands of somebody who looked after them. She particularly noticed how neatly his nails were cut. Maybe they had even been manicured.

The thought struck her that maybe he was a gambler. It certainly fitted with the way that he had cared for his hands. And even the fact that he probably had a few hundred dollars in his wallet. Yes, a gambler. That seemed to be his most likely profession.

Well, she had nothing against gamblers. As long as they paid the rent and didn't come back drunk. She had had a couple of gamblers as lodgers since her husband died. And they had never caused any trouble.

Her assessment of her lodger as a reasonably upright citizen received a sharp jolt one day when she saw him going into the brothel. While she didn't disapprove of gamblers, she certainly disapproved of brothels. And the men who frequented them.

She was torn between two courses of action. Should she ask him to leave the house in view of his visit to the brothel. Or should she ignore it and hope it was just a one-off incident?

She was forced to make a decision a couple of days later when she saw Dryden again going into the brothel. This second visit forced her to make the decision. She would definitely ask him to leave.

She did so after he had had his evening meal. She pointed out that she had seen him entering the brothel on two occasions. That she was accustomed to her lodgers being men who maintained a certain moral standard. That it was obvious that Mr Dryden fell short of that standard. So she regrettably must ask him to leave.

To her surprise he smiled.

'I don't think it's funny,' she snapped.

'I visit the brothel because I'm paid to go there,' he stated.

'Well, I think that's the most

disgusting thing I've ever heard. To be a paid pimp in a brothel.' She couldn't contain her anger. 'You can leave this house now.' She pointed dramatically towards the door.

'I'm paid by the lady who owns it because I'm a doctor. I go there to check whether the girls are clean. To make sure that they're not spreading any disease.'

Mrs Neal accepted the explanation grudgingly. 'Well, if you're a doctor . . .' she let the words hang in the air.

★   ★   ★

'Why didn't you say you were a doctor when you enquired about the room?' They were seated in Mrs Neal's parlour, and to celebrate the fact that she had a doctor in the house she had made coffee.

'There are a couple of reasons. The main one is that I wasn't sure whether I'll stay in the town. Once people know

I'm a doctor they will start asking me for treatment for various illnesses, and before I know it the decision whether to stay or not is taken out of my hands.'

'I see. So you came here without revealing that you are a doctor in order to suss out the town before you decided whether or not you are staying?'

'That's it. I just wanted some time to myself in order to go around the town before I made a definite decision.'

'And have you reached a decision?'

He didn't answer her question. 'One of the things I wanted to find out was how many doctors are already practising in the town. Maybe there isn't room for another doctor.'

'I can tell you how many doctors there are,' she replied. 'Three. And none of them is any good in my opinion.'

Clay smiled. 'So you haven't got any faith in your present doctors?'

'You can say that again. There's old Doctor Smythe. When I say old, I mean old. He must be in his seventies if he's a day. He should have given up practising years ago. He's got a young assistant, Doctor Peebles. He's Scottish. I've never been to him for treatment. But people say that he's very brusque. He hasn't got any bedside manner.'

'What about the other doctor, Doctor Lewis?' demanded Clay, sipping his coffee.

'He's the one I go to. He's in his forties. He's always busy carrying out some experiment or other. He seems to be more interested in these experiments than in his patients' illnesses.'

'Of course three doctors might be enough for the town as it is,' said Clay, thoughtfully.

'Two doctors,' said Mrs Neal. 'You can't count old Doctor Smythe.'

'The population of the town is three thousand two hundred.'

'Is it now? I would have thought it was more than that.'

'I was talking to the teacher, Miss . . . '

'Simpson.'

'She told me that at the last meeting of the town council that was the figure the council was working on. They had to know how many people were in town so that they could start charging rates.'

'I'm not paying any rates,' said Mrs Neal indignantly. 'The council doesn't provide me with any amenities. I get my water from the pump. As you know we use oil lamps and there's no running water. So what do they do for me?'

'The council are thinking ahead about what will happen when the railway arrives here.'

'Railway. Railway. I'm fed up with hearing about it,' she said angrily.

Her mood was dissolved by a knock at the door. She opened it and a pretty young woman and a young girl stepped inside.

'Hullo, Grandma,' said the young girl. Kisses were exchanged and the newcomers were introduced to Clay as Mrs Neal's daughter, Anna, and her granddaughter, Clara.

Clara didn't hesitate in finding out

more about Clay. 'How old are you, Mr Dryden?' she demanded.

'Clara, you don't ask a person their age,' said her mother, sharply.

'It's all right,' replied Clay. 'I'm thirty-two.'

'I'm seven,' replied Clara.

'Mr Dryden is a doctor. He's just deciding whether to stay in Crossville or not,' stated Mrs Neal.

'I've got swollen tonsils,' stated Clara. 'Doctor Peebles said so. I don't like him though.'

'You haven't decided whether to stay or not?' asked Anna.

'Oh, I think I have. How could I decide to move on when there are pretty young ladies like Clara requiring treatment.'

'Well at least you've got the right bedside manner,' observed Anna.

3

The following morning Clay entered the brothel named Samantha's Massage Parlour. The entrance was thickly carpeted and the heavily framed pictures on the walls helped to give it an air of respectability.

He went up to an ornate desk where an attractive young lady was painting her nails. As Clay approached she held up her hand to show him her handiwork.

'What do you think of this, Clay?' She had painted them crimson.

'You really are a crimson woman now, Norma,' he said.

'I never really understood the meaning of that,' she confessed.

'Maybe you should read your Bible more often,' he stated. 'Is Sam in?' he added.

'She's in her room. You can go on up.

She hasn't got any visitors.'

He went up the carpeted stairs. It resembled a first-class hotel with more pictures hanging on the walls — this time mainly of politicians of the past. He reflected, not for the first time, that some of the more religious ones would turn in their graves if they knew their portraits were being used to adorn a brothel.

He knocked on Samantha's door and in response to her 'Come in,' he entered her room.

She was seated on a large settee. She had been reading a newspaper, but when she saw who her visitor was she put it to one side, giving him a welcoming smile.

'Come and sit by me, Clay,' she said, patting the seat.

She was a beautiful woman in her early thirties. She was a large woman whose tight-fitting black dress emphasized her breasts. She had been admired as a beauty by many a beau when she was younger, and still hadn't lost any of her attractiveness. Her red hair crowned a face with a pale complexion, a perfect nose, blue eyes set wide apart and sensuous lips. Clay never tired of looking at her. Since he was now sitting so close to her he had the addition of the delicate aroma of her perfume to help to attract him.

'Is there anything wrong with any of my girls? You came to check them yesterday.' A slight frown appeared on her forehead.

'No, they're all clean, Sam.'

'Good. That's always a relief to hear. Have you come on business or pleasure, Clay?'

'Business, I'm afraid.'

'We could mix it with a little pleasure.' She drew up the hem of her dress suggestively, revealing more of a shapely leg.

'Don't tempt me, Sam,' said Clay, regretfully.

'Well, you can't blame a girl for trying,' she said, favouring him with an imitation pout.

'Girl?' replied Clay. His smile took the sting out of his words.

'All right. More mature lady. Anyhow, if I remember rightly you couldn't wait to get my knickers off when we were younger.'

Clay sighed. 'It all seems a long time ago.'

She produced a packet of cigars and handed one to Clay before taking one herself. He lit them with a spill from a flame produced by a nearby lamp.

'You know my offer still stands,' she said.

Clay blew out some smoke. 'To marry you and by doing so it would give this establishment an air of respectability.'

'That's right. You'd have nothing to lose. If you wanted to take another paramour you'd find it would be all right with me. I'm not the jealous type.'

'It's a tempting offer.'

'Can I tempt you some more?' This time she raised her dress above her knee.

Clay hesitated. She could read the indecision on his face. She had had years of practice in gauging whether a man wanted her or not. Her perfect Cupid's bow lips parted in a smile that suggested she had achieved her aim. The victory was hers.

'Well, what are you waiting for?' she purred.

'I'll have to think about it.'

The welcoming smile was wiped from her face in an instant. 'Well don't take too long,' she snapped. 'As you pointed out, none of us is getting any younger. As for marriage I've already had two attractive offers since I've come to Crossville. If I accept one of them I'll send you a piece of wedding cake.'

The interview was over. To emphasize the point Samantha picked up the newspaper she had been reading when he entered the room.

Clay stood up. He knew without a shadow of a doubt that this wasn't the right moment to broach the subject that he had intended to raise. He crossed the room to the door. He opened it and glanced back at her as she was studying the newspaper. There was no doubt about it: she was the most attractive woman in Crossville. He closed the door gently like a parent not wishing to disturb a sleeping child.

4

'I've found out where he is. He's in Crossville.'

The statement was uttered by an outlaw named Sankey. The five other outlaws who were collectively known to the law as the Sankey gang, regarded him with a mixture of surprise and delight.

'Well, aren't you going to congratulate me?' demanded their chief.

'How did you manage to find him?' demanded Digby. He was the sharpshooter of the gang.

'I had a telegram from this friend of mine, named Bayson. We were in jail together. He told me that he was living in Crossville and that a new doctor had arrived in the town. His name was Clayton Dryden.'

'But Clayton's name isn't Dryden,' stated Goolie. He was generally regarded as the slowest-witted of the gang. He was usually given any of the more unpleasant menial tasks that had to be undertaken.

'He tried to hide his identity.' Sankey addressed him as though speaking to a ten-year-old boy. 'What's his real name?'

'Clayton Young,' replied Goolie, without hesitation.

'As we know he was brought up by his grandparents — and their names were ... ' He paused for several seconds in order to give Goolie time to bring their name to mind.

'Dryden,' exclaimed Goolie, triumphantly at last.

'Exactly. So Clay took their name thinking that it would put us off any chance of finding him.'

'So how did your friend find him?' demanded Frenchie. None of the gang knew his real name, although he had been a member for the past six months. He always went by the name of the country of his birth.

'I don't know. He didn't send me a letter,' said Sankey, irritably. 'In the telegram he just said that Clayton Dryden is in Crossville.'

One of the members who so far hadn't entered the conversation spoke up. 'How does your friend know Clay?' He was the effeminate member of the gang. A year ago when the gang had been formed there had been some disagreement about accepting him into their ranks. But when Padlow had been given a trial period and had proved that he was an excellent cook, his place had been assured.

'We were all brought up together,' Sankey explained. 'Clay, myself, Digby, Bayson and Samantha. Bayson said that Samantha is also in Crossville.'

'Who's Samantha?' demanded Frenchie, whose interest was always aroused at the mention of one of the opposite sex.

'She was the most beautiful girl in town,' said Sankey, with more than a hint of dreamy reminiscence in his voice. 'Everybody wanted to go out with her.'

'Did you?' pursued Frenchie.

'Once or twice. But guess who she preferred,' snapped Sankey.

'Clay,' stated Digby.

'Exactly.'

'Is that the reason why we're going after him? Because he stole your girl?' demanded Goolie.

'Don't be stupid,' said Sankey, irritably. 'We're going after him because he shot my kid brother. In cold blood,' he added bitterly. 'He was fast. That's why we let him join the gang. I don't think he killed anybody though. Except my brother.' There was the same note of bitterness in his voice when he mentioned his sibling.

'So what other reason have we got for going to Crossville? Apart from you getting even about your brother's killing?' demanded the last member of the gang, Quilly. He was generally regarded as the intellectual member.

'It's the ideal town for us to work

from,' stated Sankey. 'It's a growing town.'

'I read in the newspaper that the railway is due there soon,' said Quilly.

'There you are,' exclaimed Sankey. 'When the railway gets there it means that the town will start booming. Everyone will get rich. Including us.'

The gang laughed appreciatively at his joke.

'How long will it take us to get to Crossville?' demanded Goolie. He was not a keen horserider and the thought of having to travel for several days on horseback was not an attractive one.

'I'm not sure,' replied Sankey. 'Five or six days maybe.' He appealed to Quilly for confirmation.

'The Seventh Cavalry might do it in that time,' stated Quilly. 'But for us we can add on another couple of days.'

'Right, we'll say we should be in Crossville in just over a week,' said Sankey. 'When we get there Clay will have what's coming to him. Even if it takes us a few days longer to get there, it won't make any difference. Clay won't be going anywhere.'

5

Clay had in fact settled down in Crossville. He had found a suitable surgery on Main Street. It had previously been owned by a dentist, but he had moved to a bigger city since there was a lack of customers. Many of the town's inhabitants followed the standard treatment of pulling out their teeth themselves. They would tie a piece of cotton to the offending tooth, then tie the other end to a door handle. The final act was to get somebody to slam the door shut. In most cases the tooth would obligingly come out.

So Clay inherited a large waiting-room with a smaller office at the rear. He had to give the rooms a thorough cleaning before opening up. In this he was helped by Samantha, who, hearing of his proposed surgery, sent over one of her girls to spring-clean the rooms.

Clay's next task was a less enviable one. He knew he had to visit the other doctors. What if one of them objected to a newcomer setting up a surgery?

His first visit was to Doctor Smythe's surgery. The surgery was part of the house. In fact it occupied a large front room which was tastefully furnished. A maid ushered him into the room.

'I'll call Doctor Smythe,' she informed Clay. 'He's out in the garden.'

Clay was admiring one of the many ornaments in the room when the doctor entered. He had white whiskers which contrasted with his sunburnt face. As Mrs Neal had observed, he appeared to be past retiring age.

'I see you're admiring one of my ornaments,' he said, as he came into the room. 'It was carved by the Incas. I brought it back from Mexico. I was a doctor there for several years. I didn't catch your name, Mr . . .'

'Clay Dryden. I'm known as Clay.'

'As you know my name is Smythe. Ebenezer Smythe. I've been here so long that everybody refers to me as old Doctor Smythe.'

Clay smiled.

'Won't you sit down, Clay, and tell me what I can do for you.'

Clay explained that he was a doctor who intended setting up a surgery in the town.

'Another doctor, eh? Well I think it's a great idea. I was telling James the other day — he's my partner, James Peebles — that we could do with another doctor in the town. Then I would be able to retire and devote my full time to my garden. Are you a gardener, Clay?'

'I'm afraid not.'

'Ah, well, anyhow, good luck with your new practice.'

Clay's next call was to see Doctor Lewis. His surgery too was the front room of a house. The house, however, was not as large as Doctor Smythe's, and the front room looked more like a surgery with a cabinet for the doctor's equipment, a curtain behind which a patient could undress and a couch on which the patient could lie while the doctor examined him, or her.

A maid had ushered Clay into the surgery.

'The doctor won't be long,' she stated.

'He isn't in the garden, is he?' asked Clay.

She smiled. 'No. He's just killing a chicken.'

Clay's face registered his surprise.

'The cook can't kill an animal. Not even a chicken. So Doctor Lewis has to do it himself.'

'Ah, I see.'

She left him on his own. He glanced at the bookcase where there were several books on anatomy. Also one by the English nurse Florence Nightingale. Clay took it out and was examining it when the doctor entered.

As Mrs Neal had stated he was older than Clay, being in his mid-forties. He was short and stocky with dark hair and a pleasant round face.

'Ah, I see you're interested in the latest book I've had from Britain.' He had a distinctive accent which Clay couldn't quite place.

'I'm a doctor myself, that's why I'm interested in it.'

'I'm pleased to meet you.' They shook hands. 'By the way I've heard about you. Your name is Stan Dryden.'

'That's almost right. Actually it's Clayton Dryden. I'm known as Clay.'

Lewis waved him to a seat. 'Well actually I'm Dafydd Llewellyn Lewis. But I'm generally known as David.'

Clay laughed.

'I suppose you've come to see whether I've any objection to another doctor setting up in the town?'

'Yes, that's it, more or less.'

'No, it will be great to have another doctor in town. Especially a young one. Do you play chess?'

'Yes. But not very well.'

'Great,' said Lewis, enthusiastically. 'We'll have a game some time. I'd offer you a drink, but I've got some patients coming in half an hour and a few of them can smell whiskey fumes a mile away.'

Clay smiled.

'Call to see me at the weekend,' stated Lewis. 'We can have a longer talk then. It's great to see you,' were his parting words.

6

The following day Clay was busy unpacking a chest in his surgery. It had just come in on the stage. His sister, Emma, who had been keeping it for him, had sent it.

There was a knock at the door. In answer to his request to come in, Samantha entered.

'It's lovely to see you, Sam,' said Clay, giving her a kiss on the cheek.

'If I remember rightly your kisses used to be warmer than that,' she said, perching on the only chair in the surgery.

'That was a long time ago,' he replied. He took in her outfit. It consisted of jeans, riding-boots and a colourful blouse. 'Are you going somewhere?' he demanded.

'Not me. Us.' She pointed to the work which had been going on in painting the surgery and putting up curtains. 'All work and no play makes Jack a dull boy. We're going for a ride.'

'I'm not sure . . . ' Clay hesitated.

Sam jumped down from her chair and went up close to him. 'Do I have to use my feminine wiles to make you come with me?' she demanded huskily.

'No. You win,' he said.

'It's a pity I didn't win all those years ago,' she replied, tartly.

Clay wisely decided not to reply to that statement.

Ten minutes later they were riding out of town. Samantha had added a bonnet to the outfit she was wearing and she looked the kind of perfect picture that artists were now putting in magazines lauding the advantages of going to the West.

She smiled happily at Clay as they rode along.

'Are we going anywhere special?' he demanded.

'It's a spot that I've found. It's a few miles out of town. It's beautiful. You'll see when we get there.'

Clay let her lead the way. They were now galloping in open country. This direction out of Crossville so far hadn't been fenced in so they were still free to follow which path they pleased. Clay knew that the opposite direction out of town was being taken over by the railway. Would this too, in a few years' time, be taken over by what the Indians had dubbed the iron horse?

They came to a stream and after riding alongside it for about half a mile Sam reined in. They were at a bend of the stream which was sheltered by trees.

Samantha watched Clay's expression as he looked around. After some moments he glanced at her and smiled.

'This is a lovely place,' he said. 'Thank you for showing it to me.'

'I call it my Garden of Eden,' she said. 'Although I don't know whether they had a stream in the garden.'

'I'd have to read my Bible again to find out,' said Clay, dismounting.

They tied up their horses and while the horses grazed they stretched out on the dry grass near the stream.

Sam's gaze was fixed on the river. Suddenly a fish jumped up. 'Look!' exclaimed Sam, excitedly. 'Did you see that?'

'No,' confessed Clay.

'Well, you should be watching the river,' Sam admonished him.

'I was watching you,' he said.

She turned to face him. 'You should have kept watching me ten years ago instead of riding away,' she said, bitterly.

'I'd killed a man in cold blood. I couldn't live with myself. That's why I rode away.'

'So you thought that by becoming a doctor and helping to save lives it would help you to get rid of the guilt of killing Sankey's kid brother,' she said, slowly.

'Something like that,' said Clay, picking up a stone and tossing it into the stream.

'And did it?'

'What?'

'Get rid of the guilt?'

'No. Because I feel equally guilty about leaving you when I did.'

'You think that if you'd stayed behind we might have got married and I wouldn't have taken up the profession I'm in now?'

'Something like that,' said Clay.

'Stop saying 'something like that', she said, sharply. She scooped up a handful of water from the stream and flung it in his face.

His answer was to fling a handful back in her face. Soon they were scooping up more water and flinging at each other. Sam laughed as the water ran down her face.

Clay scooped a handful from the stream and threw it over her. It soaked much of her hair.

'Why you . . . ' she gasped shaking the water out of her eyes.

Before Clay could scoop another handful of water she jumped on him.

He was unprepared for the sudden attack and instead of grabbing some of the water from the stream he ended by being tipped into the stream itself. Fortunately it was only a couple of feet deep and he managed to keep his head above water.

Sam surveyed the result of her sudden attack from the bank. There was consternation on her face. Then, seeing that the stream wasn't too deep she began to laugh. She was still laughing when Clay emerged from the stream. However her laughter changed to howls of protest when he picked her up bodily and tossed her into the stream.

It was his turn to laugh at her plight.

'Why you . . . ' This time the exclamations were accompanied by a string of obscenities as she emerged from the stream.

'Tut! Tut!' said Clay. 'Such language.' He began to take off his clothes and hang them on the branches of trees to dry.

Sam emerged from the stream and

began to follow Clay's example.

In a short while they were both naked. Clay stared at her admiringly.

'You've got a beautiful body, Sam,' he said.

'Coming from a doctor who has seen dozens of bodies, I take that as a compliment,' she said.

She sidled up to him. He put his arms around her.

'I said this was the Garden of Eden, didn't I?' she said.

'So you did,' he said, slipping down on to the ground and drawing her down with him.

'And you know what they did in the Garden of Eden.' Her tongue lightly brushed against his lips.

'No, you'll have to remind me.' He moved his body so that he was lying on top of her.

'I think you'll find you can remember it.'

'If I remember rightly it went something like this,' he said, as they began to move rhythmically together.

7

'Have you finished your surgery yet?' the question came from Mrs Neal the following morning.

'Almost,' replied Clay.

'At last you've answered a question,' she said.

'What do you mean?' demanded Clay.

'I've asked you twice whether you want more toast, but you haven't replied. But there, I expect you've got other things on your mind — what with the surgery about to open.'

'Yes, I've got things on my mind,' said Clay, munching a piece of toast.

'I've got some news, too,' said Mrs Neal.

'Yes?' Clay regarded her expectantly.

'They're going to close down the brothel.'

'What?' Clay's exclamation was so

loud that it took Mrs Neal by surprise.

'Well, there's no need to jump down my throat because I mentioned it,' she said, reproachfully.

'I'm sorry. It took me by surprise. Who are going to close it down?'

'Why the women of the town of course. They're going to hold a meeting and decide it should close.'

'But it doesn't do any harm. And the girls are clean. I've checked them myself.'

'That's as maybe. But it shouldn't have been opened in the first place. Young women selling their bodies. I think it's disgusting.'

'It's been going on for a long time,' said Clay, drily. 'They say it's the oldest profession.'

'Well they won't be doing it much longer in this town,' said Mrs Neal, positively.

An hour or so later Clay called to see Sam.

'Well, this is a surprise,' she said, with

a welcoming smile. 'Shall I lock the door?'

'I've come to warn you,' said Clay, ignoring the blatant invitation.

'To warn me?' Sam leaned back on the settee in a provocative attitude.

'Maybe you should sit by me here and hold my hand since I'm in danger.'

Clay chose one of the other chairs. 'This is serious,' he said. 'The town's women's committee are going to close you down.'

A frown appeared on her forehead. 'How do you know?'

'My landlady, Mrs Neal, told me. The women are going to hold a meeting and they're going to close you down.'

'They can't do that,' she said, indignantly. 'I pay my rates. In fact I pay extra to make sure that the town council is kept sweet.'

'I don't know how much influence these women have,' stated Clay.

She stood up and began to pace around the room. 'I've been here six months and there hasn't been any trouble. I've never had to call the sheriff or his deputy here to sort things out. There's been more trouble in the Rising Sun saloon. They're called there a couple of times a week. Why don't they close that down?' She faced him angrily.

'I don't know. I haven't been here long enough to know which saloons they get trouble from.'

'I'll tell you one thing.' She stood in front of him with her hands on her hips. 'If the women's committee think I'm going to take this lying down, they can think again.'

'I think you'd better rephrase that,' said Clay, mildly.

Her response wasn't the usual smile. She began to pace round the room once more.

'I'll fight them all the way. I've got a few surprises up my sleeve that will make them think again. Some of my clients are prominent members of the community. I'm sure they won't want to have their regular hour of relaxation

44

cut short by a lot of busybody housewives.'

'Maybe you're on dangerous ground there,' suggested Clay.

'What do you mean?' She stood in front of him again in a belligerent attitude.

'Well these . . . prominent members of society might not support you when it comes to the crunch. They'll deny ever having come here in order to save their reputations.'

'Yes, maybe you're right. What shall I do?'

'Try to find out more about this women's committee. I've got to go in front of the town council this afternoon to have my official stamp of approval on opening the surgery. I'll have a word with a few of them and try to find out more. Maybe it's all a storm in a teacup. Maybe it'll just blow over.'

'Maybe you're right. Maybe I was overreacting.' She took up her seat on the settee. 'Now I've got news for you, Clay.'

She had calmed down. She patted the settee. He came over and sat by her.

'What news?'

'Bayson is in town.'

'Oh, no!' Clay groaned.

'Oh, yes. I saw him in one of the coffee houses.'

'Are you sure it was him?'

'I'm positive. We grew up together if I remember rightly.'

'You know what this means?'

'That Sankey isn't too far away?'

'Exactly.'

'Although maybe he hasn't got in touch with Sankey yet to tell him that I'm here,' said Clay, clutching at a straw.

'If he hasn't you could always try to pay him off. Maybe a few hundred dollars will make him think twice about getting in touch with Sankey.'

'Yes, it's worth a try,' said Clay, thoughtfully.

'There's one other thing,' stated Sam.

'What's that?'

'When I was in your surgery yesterday I saw some of the contents of the trunk that your sister had sent. I noticed your guns were in it. If I were you I'd wear them before you confront Bayson.'

8

Clay decided to waste no time in trying to find Bayson. Back in his surgery he followed Sam's advice and collected his gun belt. He took the gun from the chest and slid the bullets into place. For the umpteenth time he wondered why Sankey's brother, Miles, hadn't checked to see that there were bullets in his gun before challenging him to a shoot-out. Surely it was a basic instinct for somebody who was part of an outlaw gang. It was as basic as checking that your horse had a saddle before riding it.

The only reason he could think of was that Miles hadn't expected to end up in a gunfight with him. Maybe he had thought he could insult Clay's sister without it coming to result in a gunfight. Maybe Miles had thought that he could call Clay's sister, Emma, all the names he could lay his tongue to — and Clay wouldn't challenge him to a fight. Then in the heat of the moment Miles had forgotten that he hadn't any bullets in his gun. Until it was too late.

Yes, that was the only explanation that made sense. Well, he wasn't going to make the same mistake. He double-checked that the bullets were all in their chambers before closing the revolver.

The problem was — where was he going to find Bayson? He knew that there were a couple of dozen saloons in the town, not to mention about half a dozen coffee shops. Bayson could be in any of them.

One of the things he remembered about Bayson was that he was a keen card-player. If that was the case then he could probably forget about the coffee shops and concentrate on the saloons. Which one? That was the question.

He decided to start at the far end of the town and work his way through them all. It was a pleasant morning and there were a fair number of people on the sidewalk. Most of them were women, either on their way to the shops or possibly heading for a coffee house which were now regular meeting places for the women of the town. Clay wondered idly how many of the women were against Sam's brothel and would be in favour of closing it down. Most of the women who passed him were young women and he guessed that they wouldn't hold any firm views about closing the brothel down. No, it would be the older generation who would be involved in any movement against Sam and her girls.

Clay turned into the first saloon, the Lazy Wolf. It didn't take him half a minute to discover that Bayson wasn't in it. The bartender asked him if he would like a drink, but Clay knew he must keep a clear head. He stated that he was looking for somebody and walked out.

He repeated the routine in the next five saloons. In fact he was becoming tempted to forget his original decision about not having a drink. He had decided that in the next saloon he would just have one drink. It was becoming thirsty work going from saloon to saloon like this.

However on his next visit to a saloon, the Steer's Head, he struck gold. Bayson was there!

As he had half-expected, Bayson was playing cards. He was in a card-school with three other men.

Clay waited until the hand was over. One of the strangers won the pot which amounted to around ten dollars. One of the other players stood up and went to the bar to get a drink. Another one was counting his winnings, while Bayson was relighting a cigar which had gone out.

'How's your luck, Bayson?' demanded Clay.

Bayson didn't seem surprised to see him. He stared up at Clay. He was in his late thirties and balding. He had a thick black moustache and the pale complexion of a regular habitué of saloons.

'Better than yours will be when Sankey catches up with you,' sneered Bayson.

'So you've told him I'm in town?' Clay couldn't keep the disappointment out of his voice.

'Of course I did. We've been looking all over the place for you. Clay Dryden indeed. Who did you think you were fooling? You knew we'd catch up with you sometime.'

'I suppose so. I suppose I always knew that it would be just me and Sankey in the end.'

'When he comes here it will sure be the end of you.' Bayson roared with laughter.

The three card-players showed signs of letting them carry on with their discussion. Two of them left the saloon.

'The last time I heard of Sankey and his gang they were in Hawkesville,' said Clay. 'It will take them about a week to get here. There's nothing to stop me from taking off again.'

Bayson stood up. 'I've already told

them that you are here. They should be here in a few days. There's no way that you're going to escape what's coming to you.'

'There's no way that I could have known that Miles didn't have a loaded gun,' protested Clay. 'Anyhow the court cleared me of murder. They said it was accidental death.'

'Accidental death,' snapped Bayson, angrily. 'You must have known he didn't have any bullets in his gun. From what I heard you goaded him into fighting you.'

'Then you heard wrong.' Clay, too, was beginning to lose his temper. 'It was the other way round. He goaded me into fighting him. He said that my sister had slept with every youngster in town.'

'So she had,' said Bayson. 'She even slept with me.'

Clay's self-control, usually one of his strongest characteristics, deserted him. He swung at Bayson's jaw.

Bayson easily evaded the blow. Since

Clay had aimed the blow in anger he hadn't been prepared for one in return. Bayson coolly aimed for Clay's stomach. Fortunately for Clay the blow didn't have all of Bayson's twelve stones behind it, otherwise Clay would have ended up on the floor. As it was he staggered back, trying to suck in huge gulps of air.

Sensing that the next few minutes were going to be entertaining ones the few regulars who were standing by the bar hastily quitted their positions and cleared space for the two men to slug it out.

'You're a liar,' gritted Clay.

Bayson's reply was to take another swing at Clay. This time at his jaw. But Clay had seen it coming and easily avoided it. In return Clay aimed a straight left at Bayson's jaw. The blow connected and there was enough force behind it to make Bayson shake his head, more in annoyance than in pain.

'I don't want to fight you,' stated

Clay. 'Take back what you said and I'll forget it.'

'Why should I take it back?' snapped Bayson. 'It's true. Your sister slept with every member of the gang. She even slept with Goolie — and she must have been hard up to sleep with him.'

'You're a liar,' roared Clay, launching himself on Bayson with no regard for his own defence. He succeeded in landing several blows but the fact that Bayson had kept his cool throughout the onslaught meant that he managed to land more telling blows than Clay.

One of Bayson's blows came into contact with Clay's eye. The sudden pain made Clay step back and blink rapidly to try to clear his vision. Bayson, sensing victory, stepped close to Clay and prepared to deliver a telling blow. However Clay saw it coming just in time. Since Bayson had stepped close to Clay he was in range to receive Clay's blow. When it came it was a perfect right to the jaw. Bayson hit the floor with a thud which rattled some of the glasses on the counter.

Clay stared down at him. It was obvious that he was not going to recover consciousness for a couple of minutes.

Clay went up to the bar. 'Buy him a drink when he recovers,' he told the barman, tossing a couple of dollars on to the bar.

'That was a great blow,' said the barman, appreciatively. 'We've had some good fights here in my time, but that's as good a right hook as I've seen.'

'Wait until the Irishmen come here,' said one of the regulars, who by now had drifted back to the bar. 'You'll have a fight here every ten minutes.'

As Clay went through the door he heard the not very musical sound of Bayson's groan as he slowly recovered consciousness.

9

'That's a beauty of a black eye, you've got there, boyo.' The remark was delivered by Lewis who surveyed Clay's eye with the appreciative air of a doctor who had viewed many such specimens in his time.

'You should have seen the other guy,' retorted Clay.

'I assume you won this bout of fisticuffs,' said Lewis. He went over to the sink where he began to soak a large piece of cloth in a bowl of cold water. 'I'm afraid I haven't got any steak to put on it. But this is an old Welsh remedy.'

He proceeded to wring some of the water out of the cloth. He brought it over to where Clay was seated before applying it to his eye.

'This is a piece of Welsh flannel. Back home it's used to cure everything from rheumatism to impotence.'

Clay smiled. 'I can understand rheumatism. But impotence?'

'I never understood that myself. But maybe it's an old wives' tale.'

'How long do I have to hold this against my eye?'

'For the best results — about half an hour. Anyhow it will give you a chance to tell Uncle David what was the cause of the disagreement.'

Clay hesitated. In the end he blurted out. 'The swine suggested that my sister had slept with him. Not only that but she had slept with every member of the gang. Even the half-wit Goolie.'

'And you didn't believe him?'

'Certainly not,' said Clay, hotly. 'My sister, Emma, isn't like that.'

Lewis went over to a desk and rang a small bell. A maid answered.

'Dora, will you pop over to the coffee shop and bring us back two cups of coffee,' he demanded. When she had departed he drew up a chair in front of Clay's. 'Now who are in this gang you are talking about?'

Clay hesitated for a few seconds. Then he began to relate the whole story about him being a member of the Sankey gang. And how he had killed Sankey's brother, Miles, in a gunfight. And how it had turned out that Miles didn't have any bullets in his revolver.

The maid returned with the coffees. Clay accepted his, while Lewis began to pace up and down the room, deep in thought.

'This guy, Miles, being a member of the gang, knew how to use a revolver?'

'We all did. Except perhaps Goolie. If anyone had given him a gun he'd probably end up shooting his toe off.'

While Clay sipped his coffee, Lewis disappeared into the back room. He reappeared with a Colt revolver and some bullets. He held the gun loosely in his hand.

'I wouldn't recommend using it,' said Clay, drily. 'It can get you into all sorts of trouble.'

'I wasn't thinking about using it. I was thinking about weighing it,' stated Lewis.

'I don't understand,' said a puzzled Clay.

'Is there a noticeable difference between a loaded Colt revolver and an empty one?'

'Well I don't know. Six bullets must weigh a few ounces.'

'Enough for an experienced gunman to know the difference between whether his gun is loaded or not?'

'Maybe.'

Lewis disappeared into the back room carrying the revolver and the bullets. When he returned there was a smile of triumph on his face.

'The revolver weighs thirty-eight ounces. The bullets weigh an ounce and a half. That's nine ounces. So the empty revolver is probably heavy enough to hide the fact whether there are bullets in it or not.'

'So what you are saying is that Miles didn't know that his revolver was empty

— which we all knew in the first place.'

'So we go on to the next assumption,' said Lewis, ignoring Clay's remark. 'Which is that somebody took the bullets out from Miles's revolver.'

'I'd always assumed that he'd forgotten to load the revolver,' said Clay, thoughtfully.

'You said he was an experienced gunman. The chances of him forgetting to load his revolver are on a par with one of us forgetting to take a thermometer when we go to see a patient.'

'Yes, I suppose you're right.' For the first time there was some excitement in Clay's tones.

'So all you have to do now is to work out which one of the gang's members would have wanted Miles dead.'

Clay became thoughtful. 'Off hand I can't think of any of them.'

'Well, I'll leave you to work it out. I'm afraid I've got surgery in ten minutes. So that's the end of my contribution.'

Clay stood up. 'If I work it out, I'll let you know.'

'I'll have the flannel back,' said Lewis. 'You'll look rather strange walking through Crossville with that held to your eye.'

10

The school hall where the meeting was being held was a large room which was used for several functions. In the first place it was used during the week when the local children were being taught there. There were two classes each weekday, one in the morning and the other in the afternoon. The morning class was attended by the younger children in the town — those from three years old to seven. There were about sixty of them who received their instructions in reading, writing and arithmetic from an elderly spinster named Miss Green. The afternoon class which catered for children from eight years old to twelve was taught by a widow: Mrs Neal's daughter, Anna. On Saturdays the hall was used for various kinds of meetings, such as the current one which had been called by the

Women's Guild.

There were about thirty women in the hall and a handful of men. A few of these had been badgered into attending by their wives. Others were there because they had become aware of the main item on the agenda — the proposed closure of Samantha's Massage Parlour. Among these was Clay.

He was seated in the back row, where in fact many of the men were seated. To his relief the chairwoman wasted no time in dealing with other minor matters, but came straight to the main one. She was a small woman in her forties who nevertheless had a powerful voice.

'The main item we are going to discuss is the so-called massage parlour,' she announced.

'I vote we close it.' A thin woman in the front shot up like a jack-in-the-box.

There was a murmur of agreement from most of the women.

'Hold on,' the chairwoman's voice

rose above the murmur. 'We can't just vote to close it just like that. We've got to have a discussion first.'

'I don't see that there's anything to discuss.' A plump woman who was sitting next to the original speaker spoke up.

'What those girls are doing is sinful. It's against nature.' A woman who was wearing a large hat expressed her opinion. It was greeted with another murmur of agreement.

One of the men in the back row stood up. Although it was warm in the hall he was wearing a mackintosh. 'You've got to remember one thing, ladies,' he said. 'The owner of the parlour pays a considerable sum in rates to the council. If we closed it down then all of you would have to pay more rates than you do.'

His remark was greeted with silence. Eventually the chairwoman broke the silence. 'It's a matter which we'll have to consider when we take the final vote, Mr Treasurer.'

Clay felt it was time that he spoke. He stood up.

'Ladies, some of you may know me although I've only been in your town a short while. I'm Doctor Clay Dryden. I've been hired to give a medical check on the girls to see that they're all clean and free from disease. So I'm pleased to say that they are all clear.'

Clay's statement brought several women to their feet, all trying to speak at once. The chairwoman banged vigorously on her desk 'Ladies! Ladies!' she shouted. 'Let's have one question at a time.' She pointed to a lady in the front. 'Mrs Hubbard, what's your question?'

'This was a nice quiet town before those so-called ladies came here. I vote that we get rid of them so that the town can go back to what it was.' There was a loud chorus of agreement.

Clay waited until it had died down. Then he began to speak.

'I'm afraid that that will never happen, ladies. You're forgetting one thing. The railway will be arriving here in a few days' time. After that things are going to change rapidly. I've been to towns where railways have changed them completely. It will bring a lot of prosperity to the towns, but with it, several problems.'

All the ladies were listening keenly to Clay. Nobody interrupted him.

'Two of the big problems will be increased drunkenness and a lowering of moral standards.' This time there was a murmur of apprehension from some of the ladies.

'The drunkenness will be up to the sheriff and his deputies to control. But the lowering of moral standards you ladies here can directly influence.'

His remark was greeted by noisy widespread puzzlement. Clay waited for the ladies to quieten down before continuing.

'We all know that about a hundred railwaymen — many of them Irish — will descend on the town. They've been building the railway for several months. They've been deprived of any contact with womenfolk. When they arrive here they will want — to put it crudely — women.'

This time there was an element of fear in the murmur that arose after Clay's declaration.

Clay began again. 'If I were you I'd make sure that your daughters didn't go out alone — particularly at night. As I said, I've been to other towns where the number of attacks on unsuspecting women has doubled with the arrival of a railway.'

This time the chairwoman spoke. 'So what are you saying, Doctor?'

'I'm saying leave the massage parlour alone. Don't try to close it down. It will serve a useful purpose when the railway arrives in providing a legitimate source for the railwaymen's physical appetites. It will help to keep the streets safe for your daughters. Don't be misguided into taking a big step for the sake of morality. The parlour has been there six months without any sign of trouble. I will personally see that all the girls are clear of disease. This is something that I haven't mentioned before, mainly because I don't think it's the sort of subject to bring up in a meeting like this. But if you close the parlour down I guarantee that within a few months the kind of disease you know I'm talking about will be starting to spread in Crossville.'

He sat down. His comments were met with silence. Eventually the chair-woman spoke.

'Thank you for your speech, Doctor Dryden. And for bringing up some points which perhaps we hadn't considered. Is there anyone who would like to add something to the doctor's remarks? If not, we'll take a vote on whether to go ahead to close the massage parlour. We'll do it on a show of hands. I'll just give you a couple of minutes to make up your minds.'

Doctor Lewis had joined Clay in the back row.

'After hearing that speech, boyo, I

think you've missed your vocation. You should have been a politician.'

'I lied about visiting other towns. I haven't been to one where the railway had just arrived.'

'In that case you should definitely be a politician,' chuckled Lewis.

The chairwoman banged on the desk to stop the discussion among the ladies.

'Right. We'll take a vote. Those in favour of closing the massage parlour raise your hands.'

A few tentative hands were raised. The chairwoman counted them.

'I make it nine. Now will those who are against closing the parlour at present please vote.'

This time hands shot up more energetically. It was obvious that it was the winning vote.

'I make it twenty-six. As a result I declare that we take no action at present to close the parlour.'

Doctor Lewis shook hands with Clay. 'If you ever put up for mayor, I'll vote for you,' he stated.

Clay made his way to the massage parlour.

'Samantha's waiting for you,' said the girl at the desk, giving him a big smile.

He knocked at her door, and was told to go in.

She, too, greeted him with a wide smile.

'I heard all about it from Norma. She told me you made a marvellous speech which swayed the meeting.'

'She's exaggerating,' said Clay, with some embarrassment.

'Never mind. The point is they are not going to close us down.'

She crossed to the door and turned the key to lock it. Then she lay down on the large settee.

'Come and claim your reward,' she said, opening her arms.

11

'How much further is it?' whined Goolie.

'Stop complaining,' snapped Sankey. 'I asked a feller when we stopped at Fort Munro. He told me it was about fifty miles to Crossville. We've done about twenty. So I'd guess we've got two days before we get there.'

'We might get there about the same time as the railway,' said Quilly. 'They were blasting yesterday and it didn't seem too far away.'

'So that's what that big bang was,' said Goolie.

'What did you think it was — thunder?' sneered Padlow.

'All right, that's enough,' said Sankey, warningly. 'We've got to keep cool heads when we ride into Crossville.'

'What do we do when we get there? What are your plans, boss?' demanded Frenchie.

'If my guess is right, Clay will have spotted Bayson. Crossville isn't all that big a town and Bayson wouldn't have made any effort to keep out of sight.'

'So Clay would have spotted him and Bayson would have told him that we are on our way,' said Quilly, thoughtfully.

'Yes, that's the way I figure it,' stated Sankey.

'So if Clay is expecting us, it wouldn't make sense the five of us just riding into Crossville,' said Digby, slowly.

'No. Our safest bet would be to try to make Clay come to us.'

'How do we do that?' demanded Goolie.

'We send him a note saying that we've camped outside the town and could he come and join us so that we can kill him,' snapped Padlow.

'All right, cut it out,' said Sankey, irritably.

'We'd have to have some sort of bait so that he'd come to us,' said Quilly, thoughtfully.

'That's my idea, too,' said Sankey, with some excitement. 'And I think I know what that can be. Samantha.'

The others stared at him expecting him to elaborate on the name.

'We kidnap her. Clay will come to rescue her. Then goodbye Clay Dryden,' Sankey concluded, triumphantly.

'We'll have to find her first,' said Padlow.

'It shouldn't be too difficult. Crossville isn't a big town. You and Frenchie will go in to find her. She might recognize any of us.'

'What's she like?' demanded Frenchie.

'She was beautiful. A redhead with a peaches-and-cream complexion. A big woman with all the curves in the right place.'

'I can't wait to see her,' said Frenchie, suggestively.

'You don't touch her until after Clay has come to rescue her,' snapped Sankey, 'I'm the one who decides what to do with Samantha. Remember that.'

★ ★ ★

At that moment Samantha was lying on the settee with a dreamy expression on her face. Clay was seated by her side rolling a cigarette. When he had finished he gave her the cigarette and proceeded to roll one for himself.

'Why is it that, having made love, a cigarette is the perfect conclusion?' she asked, with a contented sigh.

Clay didn't reply.

She studied him. 'What are you thinking about?'

'Sankey and his gang.'

'Must you spoil a perfect afternoon by mentioning his name?' she demanded, irritably.

'I was thinking about what Doctor Lewis suggested.'

'Which was?'

'That one of the gang took out the bullets from Miles's revolver.'

'Yes, I suppose it's possible,' she said, slowly.

'Somebody who was jealous of the

fact that Sankey had made his brother second-in-command without consulting the rest of the gang,' said Clay, warming to his theme.

'Yes, I suppose it's possible.'

'And don't keep saying 'I suppose it's possible',' he said, giving her a playful punch on the cheek.

'The question is, which one?' she said, with a smile.

'It must have been either Digby or Quilly.'

'You're forgetting Goolie,' she stated.

'He hasn't got enough brains to work out a plot like that,' he said, dismissively. 'But of course we are forgetting one other person.'

'Who?'

'Bayson.'

'Bayson.' She nodded slowly. 'Yes, it could well have been. He always was a rat.'

'But when his plan succeeded why did he leave the gang?'

'Maybe he thought the truth would

come out. Especially when your trial started.'

'When we had the fight in the saloon I should have kept on beating him until he told the truth.'

'He's still around town. He tried to come in here. But I'd warned the girls against letting him in.'

'Yes, I should be able to catch up with him before the rest of the gang arrive. If I can get him to confess, I'll be able to convince Sankey that I'm in the clear about being responsible for Miles's death.'

He tossed his cigarette into the bowl which was reserved for cigarettes. Samantha had already discarded hers.

'Now that we've finished with that, perhaps we should go to any other business.'

'What have you got in mind?' she said, stretching out languorously.

'Oh, this and that,' he said, running his hand over her breasts.

'Don't you think you should be going

out to look for Bayson,' she said, with a teasing smile.

'Bayson can wait.' His hand moved down to between her thighs.

She moaned as he gently began to caress her. 'There's always tomorrow,' she whispered, huskily.

'You talk too much,' he said, as his lips found hers.

She seized his head and kissed him fiercely.

Their lovemaking was just as fierce. It was as though they were trying to make up for all the time they had been apart in one frenzied bout of lovemaking. Eventually they both reached their climaxes. Samantha punctuated hers with sharp cries.

Clay rolled off her. He looked down at the beads of perspiration on her face and at her heaving breasts.

When her breath had settled down she smiled up at him.

'I wish I was a painter,' he said. 'I'd like to capture you now with that beautiful smile.'

'That's the nicest thing you've ever said to me.' She pulled his head down to kiss him. When she released him she said, 'Come and lie down by me. There's room on the settee for the two of us. We'll go to sleep, just like a married couple.'

She rolled over and Clay moved close to her. He put his arm around her.

'Mm,' she sighed, contentedly.

Maybe this was the time to tell her that he would marry her. There was no doubt that they were perfectly compatible. Yes, they could get married and leave Crossville before Sankey and his gang arrived. They could go to San Francisco. Sankey would never catch up with him there. It had been a thousand to one chance that Bayson had been in Crossville. They could even go to Canada. The border wasn't too far away. He could always get a job there. Yes, they would settle down together. As she said, like an old married couple.

'Sam,' he whispered

Her reply was a gentle snore.

He smiled. He decided against waking her. After all, there was always tomorrow.

12

'How long do you think it will be before we finish the job?' The remark was directed to the chief railway engineer, Tom Larson by his deputy, Ed Cotton.

'If the last consignment of rails arrives from Fort Munro today, we should be able to finish it by the end of the week.'

The chief engineer was an experienced railwayman who had worked on railway projects up and down the country, and even as far afield as Mexico.

'It will be a relief to the working gangs. Some of them are getting restless. They're missing you know what.'

'You mean beer,' suggested Larson.

'I mean sex,' stated Cotton. He was still in his thirties. He knew that Larson was thinking of retiring in a few years' time. He hoped to get the job and continue building railways before the time came when the map of America would be covered by them.

'Yeah, I guess so. I've heard that there's a brothel in Crossville so maybe it will cater for the Irishmen.'

The expected rails arrived in the afternoon. Larson and Cotton watched them being unloaded.

'Tell them there'll be a bonus if they finish by Friday,' said Larson.

One of the Irishmen overheard the remark.

'That will be a hundred dollars you're suggesting,' he said with a grin.

'I might make it as much as twenty, Murphy,' replied Larson.

'There's one thing I'd like to ask,' Murphy ventured.

'Go ahead,' said Larson.

'Say we finish on Friday, what happens next?'

'What do you mean?' demanded Cotton.

'Will we all be out of work? Most of

us are railwaymen and after living it up for a few days in Crossville, we'd like to go on to another job.'

Larson scratched his chin thoughtfully. Eventually he said, 'I don't really know what other jobs are planned for the future.'

'Why don't I find out?' suggested Cotton. 'I could ride into Crossville. It's less than a mile now. I could telegraph headquarters and ask them what other lines are being planned.'

'Yes, that's a good idea,' stated Larson. 'We should get a reply before the end of the week and you'll tell the gangs what their chances are of getting another job.'

* * *

Later that day Clay had finished his dinner and the topic of the railwaymen was raised by Mrs Neal.

'They say the mayor is going to have an official opening ceremony when the first train arrives,' she stated.

Clay, who had been rolling a cigarette, said: 'Are you going to it?'

Mrs Neal bristled. 'Certainly not. I wouldn't be seen dead with him and those councillors. You know what the mayor is hoping for, don't you?'

'No.'

'He's hoping that the town will expand enough for him to have a seat in the House of Representatives in Washington.'

'How many would the town's population have to be before he could get that?'

'Five thousand.'

'So that means it will have to go up by another thousand or so.'

'At the rate people are coming to town maybe he'll get there fairly soon.'

There was a knock at the door and Anna entered. She kissed her mother and smiled at Clay.

'You made a good speech at the women's meeting,' she informed him.

'You heard it?'

'Yes.'

'She's a traitor,' said Mrs Neal, hotly. 'She said she voted in favour of keeping the brothel open.'

'It was Clay's speech that swayed the vote,' Anna stated.

'I only pointed out that with a lot of outsiders moving into Crossville, it would be better to keep the brothel open. If not the prostitutes will be on the streets. That's the last thing you would want to see in your town.' He addressed the remark to Mrs Neal.

She shuddered at the mental picture he had conveyed.

'Clay said he had seen it happen in other towns,' supplied Anna. 'I think that is what swayed the audience.' Clay lit his cigarette to hide his embarrassment.

'I'll leave you young people to discuss the town's affairs,' said Mrs Neal, as she went into the kitchen to wash the dishes.

There was silence for a few moments then Clay said: 'How is Clara?'

'Her tonsils aren't too bad at the

moment. Perhaps you could have a look at them if I come into the surgery tomorrow morning.'

'Yes, that will be fine. I've also got a surgery in the afternoon, if it's more convenient.'

'The morning would be better. I work in the afternoons.'

'I wouldn't think there are many opportunities for work for a young lady in this town.'

'You're right. There aren't. And not so much of the young — I won't see thirty again.'

Clay smiled. 'As somebody said, there are three things a man shouldn't enquire to a woman about. And all of them are her age.'

Anna laughed.

'So what do you do?' enquired Clay.

'I teach at the school. In the hall where you made your memorable speech.'

'It wasn't that memorable.'

'Maybe not. But it achieved its purpose.'

'So what do you teach?' asked Clay, anxious to change the subject.

'Reading, writing, arithmetic and poetry.'

'Poetry,' said a surprised Clay.

'Poetry is the highest expression of mankind. I aim to get them to learn at least one poem before they leave. How would you say to a woman, 'You are beautiful?'

Clay thought for a few moments. 'It all depends.'

'On what?'

'On the circumstances.'

'Yes, I suppose so. But a nineteenth-century poet put it very well. He said:

'She walks in beauty, like the night
   of cloudless climes and starry
   skies;
And all that's best of dark and
   bright
Meet in your aspect and your eyes:
Thus mellow'd to that tender light
Which heaven to gaudy day
   denies'.'

At that moment Mrs Neal came in with two cups of coffee.

'She isn't on her favourite hobby horse — poetry, is she?'

'It's a lovely poem,' said Clay, as he stirred his coffee thoughtfully. 'Who wrote it?'

'An English poet named Lord Byron.'

'I can see my education has been neglected. I was never taught poetry in school.'

'I'll bring a book in for you when I bring Clara in to see you tomorrow.'

'Poetry,' said Mrs Neal, scornfully. 'What use is it?'

'It teaches us that there are other things in life apart from our daily, mundane routine. It's the highest expression of mankind.'

'What about music?' demanded Mrs Neal.

'Music has its place, of course.'

Clay, sensing that a well-worn argument was about to take place, finished his coffee. He stood up.

'If you'll excuse me, I've got an appointment.'

'A doctor's work is never done,' said Mrs Neal.

As Clay left the room he wondered what she would say if she knew that he intended going to a saloon to challenge a man to a gunfight.

13

Clay found Bayson in the Steer's Head, as he had guessed he would. The bar was quite crowded and Bayson was standing by it idly watching a game of cards that was taking place at a nearby table.

The barman recognized Clay. 'You're not going to have a fight again, are you?' he asked warily.

'It'll be just a friendly talk,' stated Clay.

Bayson, too, had recognized Clay. He moved near enough to hear his promise.

'You're the last person I'd want to have a friendly talk with,' he snapped.

'You shouldn't say things like that to someone who was about to buy you a drink,' said Clay, reproachfully.

'If you were the last person on earth I wouldn't take a drink from you,'

Bayson spat out.

'I'll ignore that remark,' said Clay. 'What I'm trying to find out is who took the bullets out of Miles's gun.'

'What do you mean?' demanded a puzzled Bayson.

'Whatever you may think, I didn't shoot Miles in cold blood. The only other explanations are that he forgot to load his pistol. He was an experienced gunfighter. He had killed two men — '

'Three,' said Bayson, automatically.

'So he would never have forgotten to load his gun. Or — we come to the other probability — somebody took the bullets out of his revolver. They knew that sometime during that evening it would come to a gunfight between Miles and myself. It had been brewing for days. You know the result. So who could have taken the bullets out of Miles's gun?'

'There's you for a start,' sneered Bayson.

'In those days I was quicker on the draw than Miles. The only member of the gang who was as good as me was Digby.'

'Yes, Digby was fast. Still is,' Bayson concurred.

'Do you know who I think is the most likely member of the gang to have taken the bullets out?'

'Who?'

'You.'

Bayson's jaw dropped open. 'Me? Why should I want to do it?'

'I can think of two reasons. One: there was no love lost between you and Miles. The other is that you thought that with Miles out of the way you would become second in charge of the gang.'

'What a load of crap. I've never wanted to be second in charge of the gang. You're making this up to try to get out of the fact that you killed Miles in cold blood.'

'If you're innocent of taking the bullets out of Miles's gun, why did you leave the gang straight after the trial. I'll tell you why, because your plan hadn't worked.'

'I'm not listening to any more of this.' Bayson's face had turned purple with anger.

'Maybe you'd like to put the action where your mouth is,' said Clay, suggestively, as he took up the typical gunfighter's stance with legs apart.

'I'm not fighting you,' Bayson blustered. 'You know you're faster than I am.'

'If I wounded you then perhaps you'd tell me the truth. They say a dying man often confesses the truth to make his peace with the Almighty.'

'I've told the truth,' shouted Bayson. His eyes were fixed on Clay's right hand which hovered close to his gun.

Clay stared at him for a long time, as though trying to gauge whether he was telling the truth or not.

Bayson sensed that Clay was hesitating. 'Go on, shoot me. You're good at shooting someone who hasn't got a chance against you.'

Clay stared at him. Suddenly Clay

went for his gun. A petrified Bayson didn't move. Clay's gun cleared the holster in a split second. However instead of firing, Clay spun the gun several times and slid it back in its holster.

'No, you're not worth killing,' he said, as he turned on his heel and headed towards the door.

Ten minutes later he was in Samantha's parlour. He told her about the confrontation.

'So what was your impression. Is he innocent or not?' she demanded.

'I'm afraid I've got to conclude that he is innocent. Either that or he's one of the best actors I've come across.'

'He's no actor,' said Samantha, scornfully. 'He's just somebody who stayed with the gang to benefit his own ends.'

Clay had been rolling a cigarette while he was talking. He handed it to Samantha.

'No thanks. I won't have it now.

They've been making me cough a lot
lately.'

She didn't notice Clay's expression of
concern as he bent his head to light his
cigarette.

14

The sheriff and his deputy were discussing the impending arrival of the railway. The sheriff was a large man named Clarkson, who had been active when he was younger. He had even appeared in a rodeo in Fort Munro. But a largely inactive life for several years had added unwanted weight to his frame. He was now in his late forties and had contemplated a continued peaceful end to his term in office until he retired at fifty. But now the spectre of the imminent arrival of the railway had changed all that.

'When do they expect the railway to arrive?' he asked his deputy.

'It should be here by the end of the week,' stated Stayling, his deputy. He was as thin as his chief was large. He was in his late twenties with an unremarkable face. In fact his only features of note were his ears, which were disproportionately large in relation to his face.

'It can only mean one thing,' said the sheriff. 'Trouble.'

'You mean with the extra drinking?' demanded Stayling.

'Extra drinking. Extra gambling. Extra fights. You name it,' said Clarkson.

'Extra sex,' suggested this deputy.

'Yes, there's that as well. Samantha and her girls will have their work cut out catering for the Irishmen.' He smiled at the thought.

Stayling dutifully smiled at the observation. He regularly went for what he called his bodily needs to Samantha's parlour. He could usually find a suitable young woman at whatever time he went there. But the thought that he might have to wait to take his place among a large number of Irishmen irritated him.

Clarkson's next question took him

by surprise. 'How many girls has Samantha got?'

'Four.'

Clarkson noted the alacrity of his deputy's reply. It confirmed the rumour that he had heard — that his deputy had become a regular visitor to Samantha's parlour. His face stayed impassive as he pursued the subject. 'She might have to take on extra girls.'

'Yes, I suppose so.' Stayling gave it some thought. A couple of new girls would be a welcome change. In fact he was becoming rather bored with the girls who were there. He supposed it was a case of familiarity breeding boredom. He was absorbed in his thoughts and almost missed the sheriff's next statement.

'We'll have to think of taking on extra help, too.'

Slowly the sheriff's words sank in. 'You mean an extra deputy?' There was a mixture of disbelief and panic in the question.

'Yes. I've had a word with the

treasurer and he tells me the town council could afford paying another deputy. Especially now that they're going to collect rates from the towns-folk who haven't paid them before.'

'Then I wouldn't be the only deputy,' said Stayling slowly, as he tried to come to terms with the sheriff's suggestion.

'That's obvious,' said the sheriff, irritably.

'Have you got anybody in mind?' The afternoon, which had started as peacefully as any other afternoon, was now becoming a nightmare. If another deputy were to be appointed, his future wouldn't be guaranteed. Until now he had assumed that he would become the next sheriff when Clarkson retired in a couple of years' time. But if another deputy were to appear on the scene, maybe his own future wouldn't be so secure. The new deputy would have two years to make an impression. If the newcomer succeeded in doing so then he could be condemned to remain a deputy on his present low pay for the rest of his life.

'That's where you come in.' The sheriff carried on blithely, oblivious of the time-bomb he had dropped and the anxiety which was gnawing at Stayling's mind.

'Me?'

'Yes, we're going to advertise for the post. Since you're good at drawing — you've drawn all the faces on the rogue's gallery around the room — I want you to make a poster.'

Not only was somebody coming in who could jeopardize his future, but he even had to suffer the indignity of making the poster to advertise for him.

'What shall I say on the poster?'

'Make it simple. Just say: Deputy Sheriff wanted. Apply at the Sheriff's office. You'd better make half a dozen and put them up around the town.'

'When do you want them done by?'

'You can start straight away. If we can get somebody by the time the railway is here, all the better.'

Stayling made his way slowly to the

small back room. It held his pens and paper on which he would normally draw a criminal's face. To the drawing of a face would be added a suitable reward if the criminal were to be caught. It was an occupation which he normally enjoyed. But not this afternoon. As he began his task he reflected that he would go to Samantha's parlour this evening. Normally he didn't go there on Tuesday evenings. But he would definitely go there this evening. It would help him to get rid of his frustration on hearing about the deputy's post.

15

'That's three games you've lost,' said Lewis. He and Clay were sitting in the parlour in his house where they had been playing chess for an hour or so.

'I'll have to brush up on my French defence,' said Clay. He shook his head as Lewis started to rearrange the pieces to show that he didn't want to play another game.

'Something on your mind?' asked Lewis. Although the question appeared to be a casual one, Clay sensed that there was real concern behind it.

'I'm afraid so. How much experience have you had with tuberculosis?'

'I've dealt with a few cases, although I wouldn't say that I'm an expert.'

'If I remember my text books correctly — apart from the obvious sign of coughing blood — the other symptom is weight loss.'

'And breathlessness,' stated Lewis.

'Yes, I remember now,' said a thoughtful Clay.

'Have you got somebody in mind?' demanded Lewis, keenly.

'I might as well tell you. I'm worried about Samantha.'

'The redhead beauty who runs the brothel?'

'Yes.'

'She's one of your patients?'

'Not exactly.'

'I know that you're being paid to check that the girls are clean. So you see her in your line of duty.'

'Not exactly.'

A puzzled frown appeared on Lewis's face. Gradually it cleared as the full implication of Clay's words dawned on him.

'You mean that you and she . . . ?'

'Exactly.'

'Well I must say I envy you. She's certainly the most beautiful woman in Crossville.'

'She's coughing a great deal. She

blames it on the cigars that she smokes. I asked one of her girls about her. She said that Samantha has started hiding her handkerchiefs. Normally they are all washed together since they are expensive monogrammed handkerchiefs. But lately Samantha has made an excuse that she's mislaid them.'

Lewis began to pace up and down the room.

'That doesn't sound too good.'

'Aren't there some retreats where somebody who is suffering from tuberculosis can go?'

'Yes, but they're mainly in the south.' Lewis stopped pacing. 'If, as you suspect, she is suffering from tuberculosis, then the climate here isn't going to help her. It's damp and it's changeable. If she is going to stand any chance of recovering she'll have to go down south, where the climate is warmer and drier.'

'That describes the place where we both came from.'

Lewis went to a side table. He

poured two glasses of lemonade and handed one to Clay.

'What was the name of the town?'

'Hawkesville. It's only about thirty miles from the Rio Grande. You have to cross a desert to get to a river.'

'A hot climate. A desert with a dry wind blowing off it. I think if she has a chance of recovering from her illness that sounds the ideal place for it.'

'It's ironical. We both couldn't get away from Hawkesville quickly enough. Now it could be the place which could save her life,' said Clay, draining his glass of lemonade.

'If I were you, I'd waste no time in persuading her to go there.'

'That's just what I intend doing,' said Clay, as he headed for the door. Night had fallen and Main Street was lit only by the lamps which many of the householders kept in their front windows. There was also a full moon, so Clay had no difficulty in hurrying along the sidewalk. There were only a few other people out walking in the street, mostly men on their way to some saloon or other.

The conversation with Lewis had helped him to make up his mind, not only about Samantha's illness, but also about another outstanding matter — whether to marry her. He had thought about it regularly during the past few days. Now the decision had been taken out of his hands. He'd be prepared to bet his last dollar that Samantha wouldn't go back to Hawkesville on her own. She had a stubborn streak of which he had become fully aware during their acquaintance. But if she wouldn't go back on her own then the alternative was obvious. He would go back with her. As his wife she'd have to comply with his wishes.

He didn't go straight to the massage parlour. Instead he called in at his surgery. There, he collected a small bottle of laudanum.

The girl at the desk was obviously

surprised to see him.

'Sam's in her room,' she informed him.

He went up the stairs quickly. In answer to his knock she called out, 'Come in.'

It was obvious that she too, was surprised to see him.

'It's a bit late for house calls, isn't it?' she asked, with a smile.

However the smile disappeared when she saw the stern expression on his face.

'Show me your handkerchief,' he said.

'Wh — y?' she stammered.

Clay's answer was to seize her. She resisted, but he held her in his arm while he put his hand up her sleeve. He produced her handkerchief.

He released her and held up the handkerchief. She paled as she saw him studying it.

'This is blood,' he stated. 'I'm not going to ask you how long you've been coughing up blood. You've got tuberculosis. As your doctor I can tell you that you have a chance of survival. A good chance, if you do exactly what I'm going to suggest.'

16

'Don't say we've arrived there at last,' said Goolie, with heartfelt relief.

'Why didn't you let me shoot him, boss,' stated Digby. 'That's all he's done, complain all the way from Hawkesville.'

The six had arrived in a wood on the outskirts of Crossville. They had found a suitable open space where they could graze the horses.

'If he doesn't collect enough wood so that we can build a fire, then I'll give you permission to shoot him,' said Sankey.

The others recognised the remark as a joke and a couple of them laughed dutifully.

Quilly went over to where Sankey was sitting on a tree-stump. 'I'd like a word with you, boss.'

'What about?' Sankey paused in the

act of lighting a cigarette.

'It's about the railway.'

'What about it?' Sankey struck a match.

'From the noises we heard on the way it's not far from the town.'

'So?'

'Assuming they're going to reach the town in the next few days, what will happen?'

'They'll have a party,' said Frenchie. 'Wine, women and song. Maybe we can join in,' he said, hopefully.

'Go on with what you were saying,' said Sankey, ignoring Frenchie.

'What else will they get when the railway is finished?'

The purpose of the questions dawned on Sankey. 'Money. They'll be paid,' he said, slowly.

'Exactly. Say in a few days' time they are going to get paid. Where will they get the money from?'

'From the bank,' stated Goolie. They were all listening to the conversation now.

'Exactly. From the bank. But which bank?'

'How would we know which bank?' stated Digby, irritably. 'There are probably several banks in Crossville.'

'Yes, but they'd be small banks. They wouldn't have enough money to pay the men. Their wages bill must run into thousands of dollars, since they've probably been months building the railway.'

'You've got a good point there,' said Sankey. 'If you're right then the money would be coming in from a town with a large bank, Such as Fort Munro.'

'Exactly,' said Quilly. 'The chances are that they wouldn't bring the money in until the last minute. So they could be bringing it in by stage any day.'

'So what we've got to do is to find out when the money is being brought in,' said Sankey, thoughtfully.

'If we could find out when the stagecoach is bringing in the money, we could hold it up. Nobody would be expecting it,' concluded Quilly triumphantly.

'We'd all be rich,' stated Padlow, looking up from the cooking pot where he was busy preparing a rabbit stew.

'What about Clay Dryden?' demanded Frenchie. 'I was looking forward to having a bit of fun with his girlfriend, Samantha.'

'I know your idea of a bit of fun,' snapped Digby. 'You had your fun with that farmer's wife while we were picking apples. If we hadn't got away from there when we did, we'd have had a posse after us.'

'It wasn't my fault that she didn't want to play,' replied Frenchie, sourly.

'We can leave Clay and Samantha for a few days,' stated Sankey. 'I think Quilly could have hit on a good idea. Tomorrow we'll all go into town. Quilly, you'll go with Digby. I'll go with Frenchie. Padlow, you'll go on your own.'

'What about me?' demanded Goolie.

'You'll stay here to look after the

horses. If you're a good boy we'll bring you back some candy.'

The others laughed. Goolie scowled.

Sankey ignored him. 'What we've got to find out is exactly when the railway is due to be finished. Also we want to find out how many banks there are in Crossville. Then you've got to find out which bank the money will be coming to. And when it will be coming.'

'We'll be lucky if we find all that out tomorrow,' said Digby.

'We'll try the saloons,' said Sankey. 'They're the best places to find out any information.'

'What about the banks themselves?' demanded Quilly.

'Yes, I can see us going into a bank and asking is the money for the railwaymen going to arrive here?' said Frenchie, scornfully.

'My idea would be if I went into a bank and made a small deposit, I'd have to fill in a form. While I was doing it I could ask casually if it would be all right for me to make a large deposit later in the week. The answer would be of course that there would be no problem. Then I would say that I had heard that the money for the railwaymen would be here and that there might be some delay on, say, Saturday. They would probably say that that the railwaymen's money wasn't coming to their bank. So it would be one we could cross off the list.'

'That's very clever,' said Padlow, admiringly.

'Yes, you can try that,' said Sankey.

'Why would the money be coming in on Saturday?' demanded Goolie, who had been wrestling with Quilly's suggestion.

'Where were you when they handed out brains?' demanded Digby.

'Come and get your rabbit stew,' called out Padlow, in time to prevent an argument.

17

Clay arrived early in the morning at Samantha's Massage Parlour. The girl at the desk saw from his expression that his visit was a serious one.

He went upstairs, knocked on Samantha's door and went in.

She was lying on the settee. She patted the space by her side and he obediently went over to sit by her.

Even in the few hours since he had seen her, she seemed to have changed. There were dark rings under her eyes. The fact that now there was daylight shining through the window showed him the flaws in her skin. She was paler than usual which accentuated the unhealthy redness of her cheeks.

She saw him studying her. 'I'm not a pretty sight first thing in the morning,' she said, lightly.

His answer was to take her in his

arms and kiss her on the lips.

'That's the sort of thing a girl can easily get used to first thing in the morning.' The lightness of her tone was spoiled by a sudden fit of coughing. Clay waited until it had subsided. Then he silently took the handkerchief which she had been holding to her mouth and examined it. Then he handed it back to her.

'It's bad, is it?' she demanded.

He nodded.

She sighed. 'I've been thinking about your proposition last night —'

'Proposal,' Clay interrupted.

'All right — proposal. But first I want you to answer me one question.'

'What is the question?'

To Clay's surprise, instead of answering she went over to a writing-desk. She opened a drawer and produced a thick black book. It was a Bible.

'I want to be clear about one thing,' she said. 'I want to know with one hundred per cent certainty whether your proposal of marriage came from the fact that you love me. Or was it in order to get me to come with you to Hawkesville to help to cure me of this tuberculosis.'

'How can you doubt that I love you.' There was anger in his voice.

'I must be sure,' she said, stubbornly. 'I want you to swear on the Bible.'

'I don't think that's necessary,' he snapped.

'If you won't swear, then I won't come. It's as simple as that,' she said, with a large degree of resignation in her voice.

'Listen, Sam, I was going to ask you to marry me before I found out about the tuberculosis,' said Clay, urgently. 'I'd decided to ask you after I left here the night before last. Then I realized you were ill. I talked it over with Doctor Lewis. He's dealt with cases of consumption before. He suggested that Crossville isn't a good place to live if we're hoping for a cure. The climate here is too damp. I told him about Hawkesville. He thinks it is the ideal place. It's hot, with dry winds coming off the desert.'

She stared at him for a long time. In the end she walked back to the desk and put the Bible back in the drawer.

'So you and Doctor Lewis concocted this scheme to get me to go to Hawkesville with you.'

When she returned from placing the Bible in the desk she deliberately went across to the only chair in the room. She sat on it, leaving Clay alone on the settee.

'It wasn't like that. I swear. Can't you see? I love you.' He was shouting now.

'On the Bible,' she said, calmly.

It was his turn to walk over to the desk and fetch the Bible. He stood in front of her.

'I want you to swear that this journey to Hawkesville is because you love me and not as a trick to get me to go to Hawkesville as a cure for my tuberculosis.'

She stared at him challengingly.

Clay held the Bible in one hand while

putting the other hand on top of it. He glanced at her face. She nodded.

'I swear that the reason I want you to go to Hawkesville with me is because I love you.'

Her face broke into a smile. 'There, that wasn't too bad, was it? Now there's only the second part of the plan to be resolved.'

Clay, who had walked over to the desk, turned to face her.

'You mean when exactly we should start for Hawkesville?'

'I mean when exactly we should get married. I want to get married here in Crossville. I want to show everybody in this hypocritical town that you have made an honest woman of me. I want all my girls to be at the wedding. How soon do you think you can arrange it?'

'I don't know. I've never been married before.'

Samantha smiled. Then she began to laugh. Clay sat on the settee and smiled at her reaction.

'I suppose the first thing to do is to

see a preacher,' Clay suggested.

Samantha came to sit by him.

'I think that can wait for a short while. I think the proposal deserves a celebration first.' She raised her skirt invitingly.

'Well if you put it like that, how can I refuse?' said Clay, taking her in his arms.

18

Two men were seated in a small office in Fort Munro. The office belonged to the manager of the Western Alliance bank, Mr Humphreys. The man facing him on the other side of his desk was his chief clerk, Mr Peters. Both men were in their forties and wore dark suits and waistcoats. Their main difference in appearance was that while the manager was starting to grow bald, Peters had a shock of red hair. There was no love lost between the two men.

'You think our stagecoach might be attacked,' stated Peters, with a worried expression on his round face.

'It's a possibility.' Humphreys put his fingers together as if in prayer. Peters noticed the irritating gesture. It was something his boss did when he was deep in thought.

'The money will be starting on its

journey early in the morning.'

'I know.'

'Of course it cannot go the whole distance in one day so it will be stopping for the night at the Wells Fargo staging post. Do you think that's where it's likely to be attacked?'

The manager shrugged. 'If I had a crystal ball I'd tell you.'

His boss was really irritating him now, He knew though that he had to try to keep calm. There was a great deal of money — $30,000 — at stake. Not only that but if anything happened to the money, he would be the one who'd be blamed. His boss, who wasn't noted for having a surfeit of the milk of human kindness, would see to that.

'Maybe we should put another guard on the coach,' he suggested, tentatively.

'We've got the usual guard. If we put two guards on it, then it would attract attention. That's the last thing we want to do. We want it to appear as if it's a normal stagecoach.'

'But there won't be anybody in it,'

Peters pointed out.

'Nobody will notice that. We'll draw the curtains, so that any passing cowboys won't be able to see inside. To all intents and purposes it will be an ordinary stagecoach on its way to Crossville.'

Peters suddenly had an idea. 'We could put an extra guard inside the coach,' he stated, eagerly.

The manager stroked his chin. He hated to admit it, but his chief clerk had come up with a good idea. It would give the stage extra protection. Peters was staring at him expectantly, waiting for an answer. Well, he'd keep him waiting. Of course when the bank's chief came here on his annual visit from Chicago he'd say that the idea of putting an extra guard inside the coach was his. The last thing he would want to do would be to divert any praise to Peters.

'Yes, that would be a good idea,' he said, eventually.

'I'll see about arranging an extra guard.' Peters was about to rise from his seat when the manager waved him back.

'There's still one thing we haven't decided.'

'What's that?'

'Who is going to be in charge of the coach?'

'I thought we'd agreed that Groker would go. He's young and enthusiastic. He also says that he's never been to Crossville.'

'Yes, but there's one snag about Groker going. As you say, he is young.'

Peters ran his hand through his hair. 'There are one or two other possibilities. There's Hawton or Tyler.'

'They're both married men. With families. I wouldn't want anything to happen to them.'

Why was Humphries staring at him like that? Surely he didn't expect him to go. True he wasn't married, but he had an elderly mother to support. His heart began to race as he realized that he *was* the person whom the manager had in mind.

'My mother is ill, I couldn't go,' he stammered.

'Your next-door neighbour has always looked after her on previous occasions.' Humphreys almost purred. 'It will give you a chance to get out of the office for a while.'

A couple of minutes later Peters went back to his own office in a daze. Why was the manager sending him on this mission.? Even with two guards, it was fraught with danger. The chances were that nobody from this bank had told anybody about the transfer of the money. But what about the other end, in Crossville? Somebody could easily have warned some would-be robbers that $30,000 were going to be delivered on Saturday. They would be lying in wait for the stage. There would be a gunfight and there would be only one outcome. Two dead guards and himself joining them on their way to heaven.

He opened the drawer of his desk. He always kept a small bottle of whiskey there in case of an emergency, not that he would touch it from one month to the next. If anything was an emergency then this was it. His hand shook as he poured some into a small glass.

19

'Be the best man at your wedding? I'd be honoured, boyo,' said Doctor Lewis. 'When is it?'

'The day after tomorrow.'

'The day after tomorrow? That's a bit short notice, isn't it?'

'You mean you can't make it?' said a disappointed Clay.

'No, it will be all right,' said Lewis, reassuringly. 'I'll just close the surgery down for a couple of hours. But why the rush?'

'I was with her last night and she was coughing up blood almost every half-hour.'

'That doesn't sound too good. So you want to get her down to the town you came from — '

'Hawkesville.'

'As quickly as possible?'

'That's right.'

'So what time is the big event?'

'Eleven o'clock.'

'Have you got time to have a whiskey to celebrate it?'

'I don't see why not.'

Lewis went over to a cabinet. He produced a bottle of whiskey from one of the cupboards.

'In fact I was saving this for a special occasion,' he said. 'And what could be more special than the beautiful Samantha marrying my best friend?' He poured two generous glasses of whiskey. He raised his glass. 'A toast!' he announced. 'To a long and happy marriage.'

'Thanks,' said Clay.

'By the way,' said Lewis. 'Did I ever tell you about the tradition when there is a marriage in the part of Wales where I came from?'

'What's that?' demanded Clay, sipping his whiskey.

'It's one of the advantages of being a best man. As such I'd be entitled to help myself to any one of the bridesmaids I fancied.'

Clay smiled. 'You'd like that tradition to carry on in Crossville?'

'It's a pleasant idea.'

Clay's smile widened. 'I don't think you'd have difficulty in choosing one of the bridesmaids for an alliance.'

'They're all attractive, then?'

'I'd definitely say so. They've got to be in their profession. They're the four girls whom Samantha employs in her massage parlour.'

Lewis's face registered disappointment. The result was that Clay burst out laughing.

Lewis acknowledged his friend's reaction with a wry smile. 'Well it will certainly liven things up in this town. Five prostitutes going to church. I don't suppose it's ever happened before.'

★   ★   ★

The six members of the Sankey gang returned to their hideout in the wood. They had arrived singly, the last one to arrive being Digby.

'Now that we're all here, let's see what we've found out,' said Sankey. He pointed to Quilly.

'There are three banks in Crossville,' he stated. 'As we had planned I went into the first bank to make a small deposit. Then I asked about making a bigger deposit, but I wanted to know when it would be the right time to make it, since I had heard that the railwaymen would be due to be paid soon. The bank would obviously be busy on that day.

'The cashier said that there would be no problem in them accepting my money at any time. The bank wasn't handling the railwaymen's pay. So that was the first one to be ticked off my list.'

'Why didn't you ask him which bank was going to have the money?' demanded Goolie.

'Oh my God! How much longer are we going to have to suffer him?' asked Digby.

'If I had asked the cashier which bank was going to receive the money then he would have become instantly suspicious. He would have told the bank manager. The bank manager would have told the sheriff and in no time the law be out looking for us,' explained Quilly slowly, as if to a young child.

'So did you find out which bank is going to receive the money?' demanded Sankey.

'Yes. It was the third bank I went to. It's called the Western Alliance Bank. We guessed right. The money is coming in on Saturday.'

'There's that cleared up,' stated Sankey. 'Did any of you find out anything else about when the money is going to arrive?' His question was met with three blank faces. However the fourth, Padlow, put his hand up.

'I went into one of the saloons where I started talking to a very charming man who insisted on buying me drinks. He'd already had a few himself and so he was very talkative. I said I was a reporter for a newspaper in Fort Munro.'

'That was clever,' said Sankey, appreciatively.

'I said I was writing an article about the arrival of the railway. I'd almost finished the article. But there was one part missing. When exactly was the railway going to be finished? He told me it would be finished tomorrow. The railwaymen would be paid the day after tomorrow. Saturday. I pretended to write his statement down. I believe that was the information you wanted?' he concluded on a self-congratulatory note.

'You did well,' stated Quilly.

'Right. I also found out something,' stated Sankey. 'I went into a few saloons and I was just about giving up when I bumped into our old friend.'

'Bayson,' supplied Digby.

'The same. He didn't know about when the money was going to arrive. But he gave me one other piece of information. Clay and Samantha are getting married in the church on Saturday.'

'Whew, it's all happening on Saturday,' said Goolie.

'He's right,' stated Sankey. 'After we've had chow, get a good night's sleep. Tomorrow is going to be a busy day. We'll have to plan how to get our hands on the money.'

20

'I think it's the most disgusting thing I've ever heard. Doctor Dryden marrying a prostitute.' Mrs Neal addressed her remark to her daughter, Anna.

'I don't see anything wrong with it. As long as they're in love,' Anna replied, rather sharply.

'In love, indeed. That woman has slept with more men than you've had hot dinners. What can she know about love?'

'They say in the coffee shop that she and Clay were once childhood sweethearts,' said Anna, defensively.

'I don't see that that makes any difference. She chose her way of life. It's not what normal, God-fearing folk would choose.'

Anna knew that she wouldn't make her mother waver from her strict views on sex and marriage. In which case she decided she might as well deliver her second bombshell.

'They're going to get married in church.'

'Not in our church?'

Anna nodded.

'Well!' Her mother emphasized the word like a stage actress.

'I'll make a cup of coffee.' Anna disappeared discreetly into the kitchen, leaving her mother to wrestle with this latest revelation.

When she returned with the coffee her mother was staring out through the window. She made no movement to acknowledge the cup of coffee that Anna placed in front of her. The result was that they both sipped their coffee in silence for a couple of minutes. Eventually her mother spoke.

'I never thought the Reverend Twanley would agree to such a thing.'

'It seems that he has. The marriage is tomorrow.'

'Well here's one person who won't be going,' Mrs Neal snapped.

'I expect the church will be full. A lot of the people will be going just out of curiosity. After all, she's a very beautiful woman.'

'That's as may be. There was nothing stopping them going to Fort Munro and having a quiet wedding there.'

Anna shrugged. 'Well, I'll be going to the wedding. Will you look after Clara for me? If I take her she will ask too many questions about what a prostitute does, which could prove quite embarrassing.'

'You know I'll look after her.' After finishing her coffee Mrs Neal added: 'I'm going to the market to get some groceries. Doctor Dryden usually finishes his surgery about this time. Would you stay here until he comes? Ask him what his plans are? Will he be staying here tonight and then leaving tomorrow?'

In fact it was almost half an hour later when Clay entered. Anna put aside her knitting to open the door for him. She gave him a welcoming smile.

'I'm afraid my mother isn't in. She's gone down to the market.'

'In that case perhaps you can pass on my message to her?'

'Let me make you a cup of coffee first. You look as though you could do with one.'

'That's true. The surgery was a bit more hectic than usual this morning.'

When she brought in his coffee she said, 'The town will miss you. The fact that you are getting so many patients coming to see you shows that.'

'There's always Doctor Lewis. He's an excellent doctor.'

'I know. But I always get the impression that he can't get rid of us quickly enough, so that he can get back to his beloved experiments.'

Clay smiled.

'I hope you don't mind me saying so, but it's nice to see you smile.'

'I haven't had much to smile about lately,' replied Clay, as he sipped his coffee thoughtfully.

There was silence for a few moments.

Then Anna said, 'My mother wants to know what your plans are about tonight? Will you be staying here?'

'No, I'll be staying with Doctor Lewis. I'll be trying to beat him at chess just once before I go away.'

She smiled.

'I'll tell Mom that.'

'She doesn't approve of the marriage, I suppose?'

'Let's say she strongly disapproves.'

Clay nodded. 'I expected that. What about you?'

'Oh, I don't suppose my opinion really counts.'

She was staring out through the window the same way that her mother had been doing earlier.

Why was he thinking such disloyal thoughts at this moment?

The one thing he wanted to do was to take the pretty Anna in his arms and kiss her. It didn't make sense. He was getting married in the morning and here he was staring at Anna and thinking these disloyal thoughts. Why

138

was he thinking like this? Was he having second thoughts about getting married? Surely not.

Anna broke into his reverie by standing up.

'I've got to go and fetch Clara from school,' she informed him.

He stood too. She held out her hand. He hesitated, then shook it.

'Good luck,' she said.

His answer was to take her in his arms and kiss her. At first there was no response from her. Then she was kissing him back. When she eventually broke away, she cried: 'This is madness.'

She turned and fairly ran out through the door.

21

The outlaws all slept soundly — with the exception of Frenchie. He was having erotic thoughts which kept him awake.

The thoughts focused on one person — Samantha. He had seen her while on his tour of the saloons. She had been crossing the road from her massage parlour to the doctor's surgery. There was no mistaking her. There couldn't be another red-haired beauty like her in the territory.

She looked so desirable that he stopped and stared at the surgery long after she had disappeared inside. In fact he stared at it for so long that an old lady spoke to him.

'If you want to go to see the doctor his surgery won't be open until four o'clock.'

'Thanks,' said Frenchie, automatically.

The sight of Samantha had affected him so much that now, almost twelve hours later, he was having erotic dreams about her. Would he ever have the opportunity to fulfil his dreams? He knew that time was running out for him to be able to find the opportunity.

There was one snippet of information that he hadn't passed on to the others. While he was in one of the saloons he had idly questioned the barman about Samantha. Under the pretext of pretending that he had seen her before he asked the barman where she had come from.

'Hawkesville,' replied the barman. 'Or so my wife tells me. Her information is more reliable than the *Crossville Gazette*.'

Frenchie smiled dutifully.

'And she's going straight back there after the marriage,' added the barman.

Frenchie didn't have to pretend to look surprised. He *was* surprised. 'For a honeymoon, I expect,' he said, fishing for more information.

'No, it seems the doctor is giving up his practice here. They're going back to Hawkesville to settle down. It's a pity. They all say he's a good doctor. I was going to see him myself about my haemorrhoids. But now I'll have to go to see Doctor Lewis instead.'

By keeping the information to himself Frenchie hoped that it would help him in his plan to make love to the beautiful Samantha. But time and opportunity were both against him.

Then, while they were having their evening meal, an idea occurred to him. He waited until they had all finished and were smoking their last cigarettes before turning in. He approached Sankey.

'I've got a problem,' he announced.

'What is it?' demanded Sankey.

'My horse has got trouble with one of its shoes. I'll have to find a blacksmith in town to fix it.'

Sankey thought for a few moments. 'All right, this is what you do. You go into town first thing in the morning.

Find a blacksmith. Get it fixed and meet us outside the Western Alliance Bank. We'll be waiting for the arrival of the money.'

'Right,' replied Frenchie.

In the growing dusk Sankey didn't notice the fleeting expression of relief on his face.

Now here he was, rolled up in his blanket and waiting for the first signs of dawn. Having executed the first stage of his plan he still wasn't sure how he would be able to approach Samantha. At first he had thought that the fact she was getting married today would scupper his plan. But thinking it over he concluded it might work in his favour. What did a lady who was getting married do in the morning. She would get up early.

Which meant that if he set off early under the pretext of going to the blacksmith's, she should be awake when he arrived in Crossville. He would knock on her door. Then, when she answered it, he would say, 'I'm a friend of Sankey's. I've got an urgent message for you.'

She would have to invite him in. Her curiosity to know the details of the message would be too much for her to leave him on the doorstep. Once inside, she would be like putty in his hands. She would be an unwilling partner to his desires, as had been several women in the past. The main difference was that Samantha would be by far the most beautiful woman to satisfy his desires.

On the last occasion that he had been tempted to attack a woman it had been that farmer's wife when they were on the trail. It had all started promisingly enough when her husband was away. The rest of the gang had been picking apples — they had been promised they could have a dozen apples if they picked all the apples on the apple tree. He had slipped into the house on the pretext of wanting a glass of water. The farmer's wife had given him the glass of water but soon realized that the reason he was in her kitchen was that he wanted something else. She struggled — the way they all did. Not that he minded. In fact that was part of the excitement. When he produced his knife, she stopped struggling. In no time he had finished with her. It was then that he had made the mistake. He had sheathed his knife.

At that moment she had screamed. He had been forced to leave the kitchen in a hurry. The others — realizing that they could all be in danger if they stayed — jumped on their horses. They were leaving the farm when the woman's husband and their two sons were returning.

The others had refused to speak to him for a whole day. Not that it bothered him. One thing he now knew for sure. He wouldn't make the same mistake of putting away his knife too soon when he attacked Samantha.

22

When Frenchie rode into Crossville, the town was deserted. The only signs of life were a few stray dogs who were wandering around in search of an early breakfast. Frenchie rode down Main Street towards the massage parlour.

If he had been a singer he would have felt like singing. Somehow he knew that this was going to be his lucky day. It was going to be the fulfilment of all the erotic dreams he'd had last night.

He arrived at his destination and tied his horse to the rail. The curtains in the windows had all been drawn so it was pointless trying to peer inside. He knocked at the door.

For a long time nobody answered. He began to have misgivings about whether Samantha was staying here. Maybe she had made some arrangements to spend the night before her wedding with friends. Women sometimes did that. Wait a minute. Samantha wouldn't have any friends, would she? In her profession all the women in the town would be against her. In fact it was a wonder that she had been allowed to run a brothel in a small town like this. He had banged on the door a couple of times more when there was a sign of movement inside. It took the form of a lantern which he could dimly discern through the drawn curtains.

The curtain by the door was opened.

'Who is it?' demanded a form that was only dimly discernible.

'My name is Frenchie,' he shouted. 'I've got a message from Sankey.'

'I don't want to talk to you. Or him,' she added, drawing the curtains.

Samantha felt pleased that she was following Clay's advice. Don't open the door to anybody, he had told her. Not until I come across. The advice was particularly pertinent since she had let her four girls go off for the night. Yesterday afternoon a visitor had arrived at the parlour with a rather unusual request. He wanted not one of the girls, but the whole four. He had explained that he was an Irishman who had been working on the railway. (She had already deduced his country of origin from his accent.) They were going to have a party that night to celebrate the fact that the railway had been completed. No party is complete without girls, he had added.

The remark had made Samantha smile. As a result of the request the girls had ridden off on the backs of four horses, clinging to the riders and heading for the camp that was situated about half a mile out of town. This was now why she was on her own and determined not to let the stranger inside. In fact, after her refusal to let him in everything had become quiet. Perhaps he had gone away, she thought hopefully.

The truth was that Frenchie had gone round to the back of the building. He knew from past experience that back windows were often left ajar in order to let in fresh air, especially in the summer. He gave a grunt of satisfaction when he saw that his guess was correct. There was a half-open ground-floor window.

It only took him a few seconds to push it fully open and step inside the room. He found that he was inside a cloakroom. There were several coats hanging on hooks on the walls.

His next move was to take off his boots. The last thing he wanted to do was to let her know of his approach. For his plan to succeed he had to preserve the element of surprise.

Samantha had in fact gone back upstairs to her boudoir.

Having taken off his boots Frenchie stepped out into the hall. There was now enough daylight filtering through the windows for him to see fairly clearly. He thought he heard the sound of a movement upstairs. Well, there was only one way to find out. He began to creep silently up the stairs.

Samantha had stretched out on the large settee. She was wearing a silk nightdress and a flimsy dressing-gown. She had been tempted to keep it for their wedding night. But a further temptation had been to try it on to judge its effect. She often claimed that her only vice was that she liked to wear nice clothes.

After admiring herself in the mirror she had fully intended changing into her usual nightdress, but the laudanum which Clay had insisted she took before going to bed had taken effect. She was too tired to change.

It wasn't difficult for Frenchie to guess which of the bedrooms belonged to Samantha. It was the one with the light from a lamp shining under the door.

So Sankey was in town. Samantha tried to banish the thought from her mind. She supposed that at some time he and Clay would have a gunfight to settle the feud once and for all. If it came to a fair fight she had complete confidence that Clay would win. She had seen him in his younger days. He was the fastest gun in the territory. If he had stayed with the gang he would probably have made a name for himself as one of the deadliest outlaws with a number of notches on his gun. Instead, fate had thrown them together once again. And she would be marrying him in — she looked at the clock — five hours' time.

At that moment Frenchie sprang into the room. He took in the fact that she was in a perfect position for him, lying on the settee. As he leapt on her she screamed.

23

Clay had spent a restless night. Normally he was a sound sleeper. Once his head touched the pillow he was almost instantly fast asleep. But tonight sleep eluded him.

The bridegroom had a poor night's sleep before the wedding.

He smiled at the thought. Was he having cold feet? Surely not. There was no reason for him to have a change of mind. He loved Samantha. He had always loved her. It was as simple as that.

But was it? A little voice somewhere in his head probed.

Of course it was simple. He and Samantha would be married in a few hours' time. They would go by stage to Fort Munro. Then they would catch a train which would eventually take them to Hawkesville. There the climate would be more suitable to cure Samantha's tuberculosis.

What about Anna? the niggling voice persisted.

What about her?

You kissed her. It wasn't a friendly peck on the cheek because you were saying goodbye. It was a passionate kiss. It took her completely by surprise. But then she started to respond. For several seconds they were what women romantic writers would describe as locked in a passionate embrace.

Why did you do it?

I don't know. I haven't got the answer to everything.

Are you in love with her as well?

That would be ridiculous. She's a lovely woman. She's intelligent. She's got a pretty face with lovely brown eyes. She's been a widow for four years. It's a wonder that one of the young men in the town hasn't fallen for her and married her.

Although somehow he instinctively knew that she wouldn't marry any Tom,

Dick or Harry. When she did eventually marry, it would be somebody special.

Like him.

The thought came unbidden.

It was no good. His chances of getting a good night's sleep had gone. These restless thoughts kept coming back. Maybe it was the whiskey.

He and David had had several glasses before they had said goodnight. Normally he was not a heavy drinker. But David had insisted that they should toast the bride with one drink after another.

So maybe that was why he was now sitting in a chair by his bed and rolling a cigarette.

He did manage to snatch a couple of hours' sleep before he eventually had to give up any idea of further slumber that night. He waited until dawn was breaking. He dressed and crept downstairs. He thought about leaving a note explaining his early departure. Then, on second thoughts, he realized he would see David in the church. So there was no need for him to leave a note.

He started to walk towards his own surgery. He had left his suit and the rest of his clothes there. It meant that he could change there before going to the church.

It was a calm morning. The sky was beginning to lighten as he walked along the deserted sidewalk. As he neared his surgery he involuntarily glanced across the road to Samantha's parlour. He received an unexpected shock. There was a horse tied up outside.

Surely Samantha couldn't have had a visitor last night? His footsteps quickened as he approached the parlour. He was about to cross the road to her parlour when he hesitated. Instead he carried on until he came to his surgery. He let himself in and quickly found what he was looking for — his guns.

He stepped outside. Somehow the fresh morning air had changed. There now seemed a threatening chill wind blowing. He hesitated on the sidewalk.

The dawn had changed too. Instead

of being a pale imitation of the day to come it had become lighter. In fact it was light enough for him to see clearly the man who came out of Samantha's parlour. He had a nondescript face with a beard of several days' growth which suggested that he had been travelling for several days. It didn't take a genius to work out that it was the stranger's horse which was tied to the rail.

The two men stared at each other. Frenchie knew instinctively that he was facing Clay Dryden, who had been coming to visit his bride to be. One other thing he also realized: to get out of the situation alive he would have to kill him.

24

In the railwaymen's camp the party was still in full swing, even though it had been going for several hours. The men seemed insatiable. Not only in terms of drink, but also for sex. The girls compared notes from time to time as they met after having been invited to one or other of the tents.

'Samantha will have to give us a week off after this to recover,' stated Eve.

Her friend, Norma, laughed.

The tents had been arranged in a circle around a fairly large open space. One of the men approached Norma.

'I've got a request to make, Miss,' he stated.

'Can I have a rest for a while,' she pleaded.

The Irishman laughed. 'Not that kind of request. To tell you the truth I'm a bit tired myself. No, what we have in mind is, would you sing to us? One of your friends said that you had a lovely voice.'

Norma hesitated. 'You want me to sing here?' She looked around to where most of the Irishmen were seated on the grass drinking beer out of tankards or straight from their bottles.

'My friend plays the harmonica. He's a very good player. He'll play you any tune you would wish.'

Eve was looking expectantly at Norma. Her friend obviously wanted a change from the routine of going from one tent to another.

'All right. Put a couple of the lanterns in the middle so that the men can see me.'

While the arrangements were being made a small man came up to Norma. 'I'm Harold. Everybody calls me Harry.'

'You're the one who plays the harmonica?'

'That's right.'

They had a brief discussion about the

first song Norma would sing. Harry played a few notes. The men suddenly became silent. Norma began to sing the hymn, 'Abide with Me'. Her beautiful voice soared into the night sky.

'Abide with Me, fast falls the
    eventide;
The darkness deepens: Lord with
    me abide.
When other helpers fail and
    comforts flee,
Help of the helpless, O abide with
    me.'

When she came to the last verse:

'Hold Thou Thy cross before my
    closing eyes,
Shine through the gloom and point
    me to the skies.
Heaven's morning breaks, and
    earth's vain shadows flee;
In life, in death, O Lord, abide
    with me.'

there was not a dry eye in the camp.

She sang one request after another. Her final song was 'Garryowen', the theme song of the ill-fated Seventh Cavalry under General Custer.

'Let Bacchus' sons be not
    dismayed
But join with me, each jovial blade.
Come, drink and sing and lend
    your aid
To help with the chorus.'

Many of the men knew the words of the chorus and they joined in the song.

When Norma had finished she was showered with congratulations. Many of the men who came up to her advised her to take up singing as her future career.

Everyone had been so engrossed in the impromptu concert that they hadn't noticed that dawn was breaking.

Norma and her three friends had stretched out on the grass.

'You were great,' said Eve, enthusiastically.

'The men are right,' stated Mary. 'You could become a concert singer. Why don't you give up this life?'

'I was a saloon singer at one time. But I didn't like the job.'

'They didn't pay you enough?' suggested Rose.

'No, the men kept on pinching my bottom.'

The other three laughed.

The Irishman who had originally asked Samantha if the girls could join their party came over to them.

'I've got a request, ladies,' he began.

'Not another session,' stated a weary Rose.

He laughed. 'No, I think the men are too tired for that.'

'Thank goodness. So are we,' stated Mary.

'It's like this. We haven't any money to pay you for your services tonight.'

'It's all right,' said Eve. 'We heard that you wouldn't expect to be paid until this morning.'

'I swear you will be paid,' said Patrick, solemnly.

'It will be all right. Your credit is good,' stated Norma.

'And of course there will be an extra bonus for you, for your singing. Now, if you young ladies are ready, the four men who brought you here will fetch their horses and take you back into Crossville.'

At that moment they all heard it. It was the sound of a gunshot.

'It sounds as though someone was awake early,' said Paddy.

25

Clay and Frenchie stood facing one another for what seemed like ages. But which was only a matter of seconds.

Frenchie knew that his only chance of killing Clay was to get closer to him. While Clay could undoubtedly shoot him from the opposite sidewalk, he couldn't guarantee that he could throw his knife with one hundred per cent accuracy from his present position. He knew he had to get closer to Clay.

Frenchie rightly identified Clay as the doctor who had shot Sankey's brother since he had been coming from the direction of the surgery. Clay's process of identification was less sure. What if the stranger on the opposite sidewalk had a valid reason for visiting Samantha? He doubted it, but the consideration couldn't be ruled out.

Frenchie stepped off the sidewalk. Clay noticed that he wasn't carrying a gun. His jacket was open and while it was obvious he wasn't wearing a gun belt, he did have a belt with a sheath attached. In it was a long knife. Did that mean that the stranger who was walking slowly towards him was a knife-thrower? He had seen a couple of knife-throwers when he had lived in Hawkesville. He knew that within a certain range they were quick and deadly.

The stranger had now reached about halfway between the two sidewalks.

'All right, that's far enough,' snapped Clay.

Frenchie halted. He could hardly keep the smile of satisfaction off his face. He knew that he was near enough to Clay to be able to draw his knife and throw it in one movement. More important, it would pierce Clay's shirt and travel several inches into his heart. It would be *adieu*, Clay.

Clay spoke again. 'What were you

doing, visiting the parlour at this time in the morning?'

'It's got nothing to do with you.'

From his accent Clay guessed that he was a Frenchman. Was Sankey recruiting Frenchmen to his gang now? Or maybe the guy opposite had nothing to do with Sankey after all. He resolved to find out.

'Did Sankey send you?'

Frenchie had to tighten his lips to prevent himself from smiling. So Clay didn't know for sure whether he was a member of the gang or not. That indecision was going to cost Clay his life, since it would give him an extra split second in which to draw his knife.

Clay was still staring at him, trying to decide how he could find out why he had visited Samantha.

'If you don't tell me why you visited Samantha, I'll shoot your toes off,' snapped Clay.

Frenchie knew that Clay could indeed carry out his threat. From what he had heard of the gang's exploits in Hawkesville, Clay had been the sharp-shooter. So it was now or never. Frenchie grabbed his knife.

Clay's reaction was just as rapid. He went for his gun.

Frenchie's knife was in his hand. He was taking aim when an inescapable truth hit him which filled him with a great sadness. He was too late. Clay was already firing at him.

Clay's first bullet found his heart. For good measure Clay pumped another couple of bullets into him.

Clay went over to the body. He kicked the knife aside, noticing that it already had blood on it. He searched the Frenchman's pockets, but apart from some tobacco and the makings and a few dollars there was nothing of interest in them.

He went across to Samantha's parlour. Frenchie had left the door ajar. Clay stepped inside.

He called out, 'Samantha!'

There was no reply. The silence of

the hall seemed to mock him. For the first time he was seized by a terrible dread. He began to ascend the stairs slowly.

Daylight was now edging the darkness aside. He went up the familiar stairs as he had done on many occasions. But never with fear building up with each step.

He arrived at Samantha's room. Here too the door was ajar. For a second Clay hesitated. Then, in one movement he pushed the door open and stepped inside.

The sight that met his gaze caused him to recoil in horror. Samantha was lying on the settee. Her throat had been cut from ear to ear. It didn't take a doctor to conclude that she was dead.

Oblivious of the blood he took her in his arms.

'Oh, my darling. I'm so sorry,' he sobbed.

He was still holding her in his arms when the four girls arrived about half an hour later. Their shock at seeing the sight before them was translated into four screams which rent the air and brought neighbours running into the parlour.

26

The stage with the railwaymen's money was nearing Crossville. Peters was inside with the extra guard. The nearer they came to Crossville the drier seemed to become Peters's mouth. He wished he had brought a bottle of whiskey with him, but it wouldn't have looked good if he had been drinking it in front of the guard.

'We should be there soon,' he informed the guard.

The guard, who was one of the world's worse conversationalists, merely grunted.

The only thing in favour of their arrival in Crossville was the fact that only now had dawn started to break. They had set off from the Wells Fargo staging post just after midnight, much to the annoyance of the driver and the guards. However Peters had insisted on an early start, and since he was in charge, the three had reluctantly agreed.

Peters had put great faith in his plan to arrive at the Crossville bank before any of the inhabitants were about. He would probably have to wake the manager of the bank and put up with his annoyance. But it would be worth it to see the money unloaded. The moment it had left the stage he would give the orders to turn round. Then they would be galloping back towards Fort Munro and safety.

He peered out through the curtains again. There was no doubt that they were nearing the town. The number of farms had increased and there were more cattle on them. How long would it take them to unload the money? Not long. The railwaymen's pay was all in notes — that was another thing he had insisted on. These were in four large sacks. It meant that if they took a sack each they could be in and out of the bank in five minutes. Maybe things weren't too bad after all. Even if any robbers had found out about the arrival of the money they would never have expected it to be delivered just after dawn.

'We're coming into Crossville now,' the driver shouted down.

He had already guessed that much, so why was the fool advertising to the whole world that there was somebody inside the stage? Although, come to think of it, it was common practice for a driver to notify the passengers inside the stage that they were nearing their destination. Maybe he was making a mountain out of a molehill.

A few minutes later the driver made another sound. It was the 'Wooah!' which told his four horses that their present journey was over.

Peters stepped out of the stage. It was his last movement on this earth, since five masked men suddenly appeared from behind a wall. They had guns in their hands and their bullets unerringly found the persons of the driver, the guard and Peters.

The guard inside the coach made the fatal mistake of jumping out of the coach and trying to run for safety. One of several bullets aimed at him found its target. But not before he had fired a couple of shots himself. And one of them, too, found its target, killing one of the robbers.

Sankey surveyed the bodies.

'That was easy,' he stated.

Digby, who had been examining the outlaw who was lying on the ground said, 'I'm afraid that Quilly has had it.'

'We haven't got time to bury him,' replied Sankey. 'We'll just have to leave him here.'

Goolie, who had gone to search inside the stage, came back out. 'The money is inside. It's in four sacks,' he said, excitedly.

'Better and better,' said Sankey.

'What about your brother?' demanded Digby.

'What about him?' demanded Sankey.

'We came here so that you could

avenge his killing,' stated Digby.

'Yes, I know that,' said Sankey, irritably. 'But Clay can wait. He won't be going anywhere anyhow. He's the local doctor here. He'll stay here. We'll take the money and maybe in a couple of years' time I'll come back for him.'

Padlow, who had gone inside the stage, said: 'The bags are heavy. We won't be able to make much speed if they send a posse after us.'

'It will take them all day to get a posse together. We'll be well on the way to Fort Munro by then. When we get there we'll catch a train, and they'll never find us.'

'Why don't we go to Fort Munro in the stage?' demanded Goolie.

The others stared at him in amazement.

'All right. So perhaps it wasn't such a good idea,' he said, defensively.

'It's a great idea,' said Sankey. 'We're all amazed that you were the one who thought of it. We'll tie our horses to the back. Then we'll travel in style most of the way to Fort Munro.'

'I'll volunteer to drive,' said Padlow. 'I always wanted to be a stage driver.'

'Right. Let's get going,' said Sankey. 'We're probably the richest outlaws in the territory.'

The others smiled at his joke.

27

The town of Crossville woke up to the news that the bank had been robbed. The exact details were conveyed by a cleaner who had been in the bank at the time and had witnessed the whole scene.

'It was horrible! Horrible!' she recited dramatically to the deputy sheriff who had been among the first to arrive on the scene. 'The stage drew up. The next thing I knew five men appeared from behind that wall there.' She pointed a finger at the nearby wall. 'They shot the three men in cold blood. Those are the three.' She indicated the corpses, now discreetly covered by blankets.

'Then who are the other two men?' The deputy indicated the corpses who were some distance away from the others.

'I'm coming to that,' she replied rather irritably, having had her story stopped while she was in full flow. 'There was still one person left inside the stagecoach. He jumped out and tried to run towards those trees.' She pointed to the trees. 'But the robbers shot him before he could reach them.'

The deputy didn't interrupt her this time. He waited for her to conclude her story.

'But that man managed to shoot one of the robbers before he died. That's him.' She pointed to Quilly's corpse.

'So then the four robbers rode away with the money?'

'I can see you'll never become a sheriff,' she said, tartly. 'If you look around you'll see there's something missing.'

The deputy's gaze took in the five corpses. He was on the point of asking her what was the missing item when it suddenly dawned on him.

'The stagecoach!' he exclaimed, excitedly.

'Exactly. They went off in the stagecoach. First, though, they tied their horses to the back.'

'So they started back towards Fort Munro in the stagecoach?'

'That's right. They couldn't have been gone an hour. I stayed inside the bank for a good ten minutes before I started raising the alarm in case they came back. If you start now you should catch them before they reach the Wells Fargo stage halt. You could ride faster on your horse than a stagecoach can travel.'

'What! Are you mad?' the deputy almost shouted. 'I'd only be one against four.'

'But it's your job, isn't it?'

'Not to get killed it isn't,' he snapped.

'You mean you're going to let them get away?' There was massive disappointment in her tones.

'I'll get a posse together. We should be able to catch them before they reach Fort Munro.'

'Pigs might fly,' she retorted, as she turned back towards the bank.

In Doctor Lewis's house Clay was sitting with his head in his hands. Two of Samantha's girls had insisted on accompanying him there. The other two had gone to see about the funeral arrangements.

'Nothing I can say can make any difference,' said David, as he poured two generous measures of whiskey. 'I felt the same way that you are feeling now when my mother died. I thought it was the end of the world.' He handed the glass to Clay. 'I've got one piece of information for you, though.'

'What is is?' A haggard-looking Clay glanced up at him.

'It's about the outlaw's brother whom you shot in Hawkesville.'

'Oh, that,' said Clay, indifferently.

'You didn't shoot him in cold blood as you thought. He committed suicide.'

'What do you mean?' demanded Clay, irritably. 'He couldn't have committed suicide. I shot him. I even had witnesses to prove it.'

'Oh, I know that technically you killed him. But we were wrong about the reason why there were no bullets in his gun. It wasn't somebody else who took the bullets out. He took them out himself.'

'Why would he do such a stupid thing as that?'

'A couple of days ago I came upon the answer. I sent a telegram to the sheriff in Hawkesville. Yesterday he sent me a reply. I intended to show it to you last night, but after we'd had a few whiskeys I forgot about it. Anyhow, here it is.' He handed Clay a telegram.

Clay read it. 'Your assumption that Miles Sankey had cancer is correct. I spoke to his doctor, Doctor Fenton. He confirmed that Miles had only a few weeks to live. I hope that this is the information you required.'

Clay read it a second time.

'So you see. Rather than face a terrible end to his life with excruciating pain he decided to end it. He goaded you into having a gunfight with him. He knew you were a crack shot and would kill him with one bullet. So that's how he chose to end his life.'

'So Miles had cancer,' said Clay, slowly.

'I could send Doctor Fenton a telegram if you like, to confirm it.'

'No, that won't be necessary. I know Doctor Fenton. He's a good doctor. He wouldn't have made a mistake with the diagnosis.'

'So that should help you to get rid of the guilt that you've been carrying around that you were responsible for Miles's death.'

'Yes, it should, shouldn't it? Thanks for finding out for me.'

'Think nothing of it. That's what friends are for.'

He crossed to the cabinet and poured two more whiskeys. At that moment there was a knock at the front door. David left the room to answer it.

There was a hurried conversation. When he returned there was a pensive frown on his face.

'It seems that your ex-outlaw gang have been busy. They've just robbed the bank,' he announced.

'So the man I killed was one of the gang,' said a relieved Clay, having had his doubts about Frenchie's identity removed.

'Apparently they've gone off with all the money that was due to be paid to the railwaymen.'

'Did the lady you were just talking to say how many of the gang there were?'

'She said there were five, but one of the gang was killed when they were attacking the bank. They went off in the stagecoach that brought the money to the bank.'

'So there are four,' said Clay, thoughtfully. 'They will probably be Sankey, Digby, Goolie and one other.'

'It's nothing to do with you now. They're probably well on their way to Fort Munro.'

To David's surprise Clay stood up. 'Thanks for finding out about Miles,' he said.

'You've already thanked me for that. And you haven't drunk your whiskey,' David said casually. Suddenly realization hit him. 'You're going after the outlaws?'

'If they're on their way in a stage-coach I should have a good chance of catching them before they reach Fort Munro.'

'Can't I say anything to make you change your mind?' David opened his arms in a vain appeal heavenwards.

'Could you see about the funeral arrangements for Samantha?'

'Why are you going? It's got nothing to do with you now.'

'If the gang hadn't come here looking for me then Samantha would be alive now. So I'm partly responsible for her death.'

'But one against four? You're bound to be killed.'

'Maybe I'm taking the same way out that Miles took,' said Clay, as he went out through the door.

28

Clay hurried along the sidewalk to his own surgery. Although it was still early there were a few people about. Some of them acknowledged him as they passed, obviously not aware of his personal tragedy.

He would have liked to start on his journey straightaway, but he knew that first he had to feed and water his horse. While he waited he checked his gun and made sure that he had enough bullets in his gun belt.

He was about to go to the back of the building to see whether his horse was ready when there was a knock at the door. At first he was tempted to ignore it. Then, realizing that it must be something important for somebody to call at this hour of the morning, he opened it. Anna stood there.

'Well, aren't you going to invite me

in?' she demanded.

'Is it something serious?' he demanded, when they were inside. 'Is it Clara?'

'No, it's not. But it is serious. I've just been to see Doctor Lewis. I thought you'd be there. He told me that you intend going after the outlaws.'

'That's right.' They were seated facing one another on the two chairs in his surgery.

'But why? It's all over now. I'm truly sorry that Samantha has been murdered. But you killed the man who murdered her. So surely it's all over?'

'As I told David, it won't be over until I kill Sankey. He came here to kill me. If the gang get away, when they have lost all their money they will be back.'

'But anything can happen in that time,' she protested. 'They could have been caught by bounty hunters, for example.'

'Sankey will be back,' stated Clay, stubbornly. 'This isn't the end.'

'It will be the end of you, if you go after the four of them,' said Anna, bitterly.

They stared at one another as if trying to read each other's thoughts. Eventually Anna said, 'Is there anything I can say that will make you change your mind?'

'No,' replied Clay, positively.

'I wasn't going to say this. In fact, I wasn't going to get up early to find out what was happening after I heard the gunshots when the bank was robbed. But here I am. I realize I've got to say what I have to.'

'What is it, Anna?' There was a more gentle note in Clay's voice for the first time.

'It's difficult for me to say it.' She wasn't looking at him now but was gazing down at her hands in her lap. 'I've never said it since my husband died — but I love you.' She almost whispered the emotive words.

'Don't say any more, please.' He put his hand over her mouth.

She pulled his hand away. 'Just let me finish.' Her voice had become stronger again. 'I've loved you from the first time we met in my mother's house. That's why I let you kiss me. I don't think I'd be wrong if I said that for a few seconds you realized that you loved me.'

'As you said, it was a moment of madness.'

'Was it?' She was gazing at him with the same intensity as before. 'Whether or not it was, we could have the chance to find out.'

'What do you mean?'

'If you will give up this foolish desire for revenge you can come to live with me and Clara.'

Her words took him by surprise. He stood up. 'Do you know what you are saying?'

'Yes, I've said it. And now God help me.' She stood too.

Clay crossed to her and held her in his arms. 'If you do that, you will be banished from society in the town. You will be living in sin. You will lose your job as a teacher. People will avoid you when you are out shopping. This is a narrow-minded town. You will become an outcast.'

'I know. But I'm willing to do it because I love you.'

'You will do this for me?' said Clay, tenderly, as he touched her cheek. She seized his hand.

'Say that you will come with me now.'

He drew away.

'So that's your answer, is it?' she said, bitterly.

'I could never accept your love on those terms,' he said. 'The price you would pay is too high. Maybe when all this is over, we can come to a better arrangement.'

'I suppose there'll always be some-body between us. Samantha,' she said bitterly as she began to walk towards the door.

She was stopped by Clay's next words. 'Samantha was going to die anyhow. It was only a matter of time.

She had incurable tuberculosis. It had gone too far.'

'I'm so sorry.' She paused by the door. 'I'm not a person who goes to church regularly. But I'll be going today — to pray that you return safely to me and Clara.'

She closed the door gently behind her.

29

The regular rhythm of his horse's hoofs on the well worn road to Fort Munro seemed to be beating out a phrase. What was it? He struggled to identify it. Then it came to him in a flash. The phrase was *don't go on*. The horse's hoofs seemed to be beating it out over and over again. *Don't go on*.

This was foolish. He knew he had to go on. As he had explained to Anna, the struggle wasn't over. At some time in the future Sankey would come back to get him.

He allowed his imagination to stray. Suppose that in a year or two he was married to Anna. One day Clara would come running into the house, and cry. 'There are some men riding up. They look like nasty men to me.'

That's how it could end. That was why he had to make sure that it ended soon. So that he could come back alive to Anna and Clara.

Why was he thinking about coming back alive? When he had left David's surgery he had been perfectly willing to accept that his life would probably end when he confronted the four outlaws. In fact the thought hadn't particularly bothered him. So what had made him change his mind?

Anna. It was as simple as that. When she had made her declaration of love it had stirred an equal response in him. He knew that if he had confessed it openly to her then his resolve to catch up with the outlaws would have melted. It would have been easy for him to have taken her in his arms there and then. He could have gone with Anna and they would have been living in sin, as Anna's mother would probably put it. It wouldn't have bothered him too much. He was used to accepting life's slings and arrows. But it would have had a devastating effect on Anna. That was why he could never accept her terms.

These thoughts occupied his mind as his horse covered the miles to the Wells Fargo staging post. He had a vague idea that he should soon be catching up with the stagecoach. How many miles had he covered already? At least half a dozen. The sun was now high in the sky, which supported his supposition that the stagecoach shouldn't be too far ahead of him.

In fact it was an hour or so later when at last he spotted the stagecoach ahead. He noticed at once there was one thing in his favour. There was only the driver on top of the coach. There was nobody riding shotgun.

The first inkling that Padlow had that things weren't going according to plan was when a man on a horse was suddenly riding alongside the coach. Instead of overtaking the coach the man kept pace with it.

Padlow's worst fears were confirmed when the man said, 'Is this the stagecoach with the railwaymen's money inside?'

Padlow recognized trouble when he saw it. This was trouble with a capital T. He went for his gun, which was in his holster.

The stranger's gun was in *his* holster, too. But the speed with which he drew it and fired at Padlow meant there could only be one end to the duel. Padlow slumped down in his seat.

The horses were used to travelling along this route — they had travelled along it dozens of times before. So they carried on, even though the reins had slackened when Padlow died.

Clay went to the back of the coach. He had noticed when catching up with it that the curtains were drawn. So the three men inside couldn't see what he was up to. They couldn't see that he was cutting the ropes which were tying the four horses to the coach. To celebrate their newfound freedom the horses whinnied as they happily galloped away.

'Did you hear that?' demanded Sankey.

'What was it, boss?' asked Goolie.

'It sounded like our horses.'

Sankey drew back the curtains to investigate the matter. He received one of the biggest shocks of his life when he saw a rider a few yards away.

'It's bloody Clay,' he cried.

The three men went for their guns. Clay rode further away and to the front of the coach so that he would be out of their line of fire.

However the three men inside, having smashed the windows, tried to get a lucky shot at Clay. The hail of bullets produced an unexpected result. None of them touched Clay. But the sudden cacophony of sound startled the horses. The result was that they started to gallop madly.

The coach was soon swaying from side to side as the horses continued with their mad gallop. Clay had difficulty in keeping up with them. In fact he was several yards behind them when one of the gang, having decided that it was better to take his chance and face Clay than be crushed to death in an overturned coach, jumped out.

He rolled several times on the grass. As he rolled he produced his gun. He was concentrating on getting away from the coach, so it took him a moment to realize exactly where Clay was. In that split second Clay shot him.

'Goodbye, Digby,' he said.

The coach was still hurtling along. In fact it had now left the road and was travelling along on the grass at breakneck speed. There was a stand of trees and it was heading straight for it. Everything seemed to happen at once. The horses somehow managed to get out of the shafts. First the front two galloped off. Then the other two, realizing that their freedom, too, was in sight, also galloped away. The coach, with no one to control it, smashed into the trees towards which it had been heading.

Clay heard the sound of an unearthly scream from inside the coach as the splintering of the coach's woodwork tried to hide it.

Clay had to wait several seconds before a figure crawled out of the crushed door. It was Sankey.

His face was covered with blood, but Clay noticed that he seemed to be moving reasonably well as he stretched himself upright.

As he did so he went for his gun, hoping to catch Clay unawares.

However, since he was already watching him closely, Clay too went for his gun.

Although the two shots sounded as one, it was Sankey who collapsed with a bullet in his heart.

Clay dismounted and approached the coach. He managed to push open the door and crawl inside. The was a figure sprawled on the floor. It didn't take Clay long to ascertain that Goolie was dead. Probably as a result of a broken spine when the coach hit the trees.

★ ★ ★

It was later in the afternoon when Clay rode up to the chapel of rest. He had been to visit the sheriff.

'We didn't expect to see you come back alive,' stated the sheriff.

Clay explained about the gunfight and where the outlaws' bodies could be found.

In the chapel of rest Clay could see an open coffin. He stepped slowly across to it. It was Samantha's. She was lying there as if asleep. The cut in her neck had been tastefully covered by a high-necked jumper.

He began to recite.

'She walks in beauty, like the night
of cloudless climes and starry
     skies;
And all that's best of dark and
     bright
Meet in her aspect and her eyes;
Thus mellow'd to that tender light
Which heaven to gaudy day
     denies.'

He bent down and kissed her on the lips.

Anna had arrived, unnoticed, and was standing by the door. 'That was beautiful, Clay,' she stated, as he came towards her. When they were outside she took his arm.

'I think that Clara is waiting for us,' she said.

They walked arm-in-arm on the sidewalk.

'It's all over now, isn't it?' She sought confirmation.

'It's all over now,' he affirmed. 'According to the sheriff I'll be entitled to receive hundreds of dollars in bounty money. Probably as much as a thousand.'

'Then you'll be rich,' she said, glancing up at him.

'I'll want it to build a hospital. It's the one thing that's lacking in Crossville.'

There was a contented smile on her face as she opened the gate to her mother's house.

A figure came dashing out through the door. It was Clara.

'Clay! Clay!' she cried as she jumped up into his arms. 'How many men did you kill?'

'That's not a suitable question to ask your prospective stepfather,' he replied.

THE END

We do hope that you have enjoyed reading this large print book.

Did you know that all of our titles are available for purchase?

We publish a wide range of high quality large print books including:
Romances, Mysteries, Classics General Fiction Non Fiction and Westerns

Special interest titles available in large print are:
The Little Oxford Dictionary Music Book, Song Book Hymn Book, Service Book

Also available from us courtesy of Oxford University Press:
Young Readers' Dictionary (large print edition) Young Readers' Thesaurus (large print edition)

For further information or a free brochure, please contact us at:
**Ulverscroft Large Print Books Ltd., The Green, Bradgate Road, Anstey, Leicester, LE7 7FU, England.
Tel:** (00 44) **0116 236 4325
Fax:** (00 44) **0116 234 0205**

Other titles in the
Linford Western Library:

A TOWN CALLED TROUBLESOME

John Dyson

Matt Matthews had carved his ranch out of the wild Wyoming frontier. But he had his troubles. The big blow of '86 was catastrophic, with dead beeves littering the plains, and the oncoming winter presaged worse. On top of this, a gang of desperadoes had moved into the Snake River valley, killing, raping and rustling. All Matt can do is to take on the killers single-handed. But will he escape the hail of lead?